LUGGALOR'S LENSES

W. S. FULLER

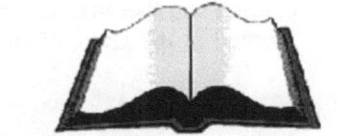

CCB Publishing
British Columbia, Canada

Luggalor's Lenses: A Novel of Insight

Copyright ©2009 by W. S. Fuller
ISBN-13 978-1-926585-70-3
First Edition

Library and Archives Canada Cataloguing in Publication

Fuller, W. S.
Luggalor's lenses : a novel of insight / written by W. S. Fuller.
ISBN 978-1-926585-70-3
I. Title.
PS3606.U5537L84 2009   813'.6   C2009-906862-1

Cover Art: Anna McBrayer

Publisher: CCB Publishing
              British Columbia, Canada
              www.ccbpublishing.com

For Parker and Finley…and Their Futures

"Blessed are the Peacemakers, for They Shall be Called
Children of God" *Matthew 5:1-9*

Preface

I first wrote about Luggalor years ago, for a literary contest sponsored by Ted Turner, one of the world's great philanthropists. The challenge was to write a work of fiction which "illuminates the problems that face the planet and its' inhabitants, and offers positive, creative solutions." The story continues...

The only man ever to walk the earth with the power to live forever lies encased in the sterile somber of this damned hospital room, tubes jutting from his body cavities, needles from his limbs, the eerie silence broken only by the steady beeping of the monitors. Larry Luggalor is going to die. And soon. And by his own choosing.

As I sit, and watch, and listen, everything so still that my breathing sounds like collapsing bellows, the remarkable story I heard over two long evenings many years ago comes flooding back. Will it die with him? Am I the only one with the strength, or weakness, to know? Could I ever summon the courage to be the messenger?

He was in one sense only one man, relatively insignificant and unaccomplished in the eyes of the world, one of those who never get their fifteen minutes of fame. But he had, of course, been everyman, and the first with no need for the qualifier 'in essence'. Then he decided he wouldn't be any longer.

He told me he had a sense he could trust me, that I just might believe him, on that evening long ago, with the hot embers of the camp fire warming us against autumn's first frost. I took it as a compliment until the weight of it began to descend. Then I looked at the shadows of the flames playing across his face and thought he was mad, and would have to consider me so, to entrust me with such a tale. But he was right, as always. It didn't take long. Believe him I did.

Many of the details of his stories I remember vividly. Better than the details of my own life. By design? To enable me to do what? The three slender, battered leather journals he had entrusted to me lie on the footstool beside my chair. Reaching down, I pick up the first one, and with the steady pulse of the soft beeps setting a rhythm for the verses of his story, I start. If I should ever want to reveal the content, or need to, if this is somehow in my destiny, I should rehearse. To know how it would flow. To feel my passion. To guess my chances.

As I think back to that first night, watching as he occasionally poked and stirred the fire with the long stick he constantly twirled in his hands, I remember how furrowed his brow had become. There was an intensity in his voice as he hunched his shoulders forward. A stress seemed to radiate through his body. How remarkable his memory was. Every detail - of word, and deed, and thought. Every single thought. That was where the weight was. Including his own, a window into every thought of each and every one of the players of his saga. The world's saga.

He started that night by the fire by giving me a place and a year. It was the same with the first page of the first journal.

1995

NORTHWEST TERRITORIES

The sharp explosion of the rifle shattered the still, frigid air, the mother collapsed in a heap and her babies instantly panicked, their eyes going wide and wild. Clubs at their sides, the Camuit started toward the brood. Wading into the middle of the eight or so small pups, they raised their crude weapons, and the slaughter began. What a strange, incongruous scene...the stunning beauty of the brilliant white landscape set against an endless depth of cobalt blue sky and what had been the stark quietness of the Arctic wilderness...violated by the sights and sounds of violence and death. The tiny Harp seals screamed as they were pummeled. A dreadful red crept into the snow around them.

"Jesus, only a few small ones. This must be only the beginning if it is to be a good day. We will be behind if this is the best we can do on the first day." Hinte was the leader and shouted to the others his feelings on the hunt, their prospects for the next kill, the weather, the plight of the tribe, and where they would all spend eternity if they could not provide for the village in the same fashion as their ancestors did. He continued to swing his club as he shouted. Suddenly there were no more screams. Silence again, except for the crunch of boots on the snow. It had taken only a few minutes, yet it seemed to last forever. Four small, beautiful creatures, lovable in their white coats, with their round, streamlined bodies and large, sad eyes...silenced forever. And their mother, also dead. Li felt a tear freeze on his cheek as he covered the lens of the camera.

What was surely one of the most elegant families on this planet, destroyed in one brutal span of mere moments for the purpose of feeding and clothing the same species that have sent their own to the moon. I could feel the passion...see it in their thoughts and actions. The same event...viewed so differently by creatures of the same species. For the hunters...pride and joy. For the photographer...sorrow and frustration. I, Luggalor.

1995

THE MEDITERRANEAN

The temperature remained close to one hundred degrees at 1 a.m. As Kabril lifted the rubber boat by the handholds on the side and began the descent down the steep bank, he felt cooler air rise to meet them from the sea. Moving quickly, he fought to keep his feet under him, leaning back so his body would not get ahead of his legs and pitch him forward. The boat slipped quietly into the surf and the three black-clad men were in it in an instant. Out past the small breakers the water was flat, and within seconds they were into their routine pulls on the oars. Aided by the rip tide they knew would assist them, the small craft moved south. Rather than tension, Kabril felt the familiar calm and peace he had grown accustomed to at the start of a mission. Many years ago, the first time, his heart had pounded furiously. Now it will only pound at the end.

"0108," whispered Simon, "we should arrive at 0430"

A long time to row, and think, mused Kabril. He liked this time of calm, of being in total control. It came from experience, of course, but he knew it also came from the endless sorrow and pain over the years. Immune to the fears of most men, having suffered so much and seen so many others suffer...there was no threat, no danger, no matter how grave, that could touch him. A shell of a man, he had few emotions left. There simply wasn't anything to hurt, or lose. He sensed the faint stirrings of an inward smile, perhaps a hint of the old cockiness. It didn't happen often. It felt good.

Rowing steadily, his mind clear, his oar slicing silently through the rippled surface, pulling with raw power through the dark sea,

Kabril remembered the stories his father told and the lessons he wanted his sons to learn. His grandfather was a shop owner and merchant in Jerusalem, in the old city , and his father and uncle helped with the shop and traveled to buy the silk and fine linens. They would inherit the business and carry on in the tradition of fortunate families such as his own. Not that they were wealthy. Far from it, but the business was strong and growing, and his grandfather was well-liked and respected in the community, and that was all that a man could ask for other than health and sons. Then they lost everything during the occupation and war, and were forced to flee the city.

"How can the world sit by and let such a thing happen," Father would say. "Good, law-abiding, devout people who have been on land that is rightfully theirs for centuries. People who pay their taxes, help others...people who have not raised a hand against their aggressors... how can this happen? How can countries that are free, so-called democracies, with laws based on high ethical standards and human rights...how can they watch, even condone those who seize our property, defile our sacred shrines, ruin our lives?"

Grandfather was a broken man when he arrived in Lebanon. He quickly became a hateful man as his family was forced to endure the camps. One of the first to join al-Fatah when it was formed, he was discouraged from taking part in operations because of his age. But when the war started he was gone in a matter of hours, and like many others, never came back.

Father had resisted being other than a vocal supporter because of the pleadings of our mother. Their arguments became more heated and numerous after Grandfather was killed, but mother's tearful references to the endless slaughter with no change, only more orphans, usually ended the discussion.

By my twenty-fifth birthday we had established a small grocery shop. My brother Nabul and I worked alongside our father and it was at this time he began to leave in the evenings, would sometimes be away for days at a time. Mother begged him to give up whatever he was doing, and of course she knew what that was. She made Nabul and I swear we would never become involved. We questioned our father but he made it clear he would explain nothing to us. We were to mind the shop and our families. He told us our time would come. Keeping us in the dark brought him some relief from mother's tirades, and he needed that.

Nabul and I also knew what was going on. We knew where the bunkers were, where the meetings took place and where the training exercises were held.

The invasion did not affect the village that much for the first few days. Many of the fighters were gone, and the shops were busy with people stocking up, but the pace was still measured, almost serene. And then the air and artillery strikes began. From the first days the injuries and suffering were horrific, the mourning of the dead heart-rending. I have never been able to recall exactly, but it was in the second week when the house was hit. Father was there - he had only been home for a few hours, and died along with Galena and my two daughters. The two most beautiful daughters in the world. I'll always see their small, broken bodies, with the perfect faces that I knew would never smile or speak to me again. I knew it, but I also knew I could not comprehend it. Remembering the total, paralyzing horror still causes me to feel a suffocating grip of panic, a sense that my body, mind and soul is coming apart, changing form, that my life is draining from me as it did that day.

I was afraid when I went to tell Mother I was leaving for training. Her blank stare, her silence...I'll never forget. But as I turned to leave I saw what I thought might be a trace of understanding on her face.

"Something in the water at 33.03 north 35.06 east, moving south, slowly, no light, no sound", crackled the voice over Major Mark Engen's phone. Engen knew the coordinates by heart."Gate AA, row 1, seat 1" he said to his driver. The jeep accelerated, the personnel carrier behind them following in close pursuit.

Engen was on patrol that night to observe. This wasn't a major's normal duty, but he liked to keep up with what was happening in the field, and an occasional, unannounced ride was a good way to accomplish this and boost morale. Soldiers like to have commanders who are not above spending time in the trenches.

"Looks like you might get lucky tonight, sir," said private Rosen." It's about time we had some action. It's been really quiet."

"That's when it comes, private, when it's quiet."

Mark Engen thought about when he last looked forward to a fight. The change started a number of years ago during the invasion of Lebanon. Before that he hated all Palestinians and, he guessed, all Arabs. That was the company line, at least in the military. In many families you grew up learning to hate, and then you joined the army and they made sure you didn't let up. The early actions hadn't really changed any of this. Seeing death and suffering, even killing, could be handled as long as the enemy was scum...as long as they were trying to kill you, take your land. But when the casualties were civilians... women and children and old people, it was different. Sure, they had done the same in many raids, but it no longer seemed to make sense, this eye-for-an-eye of innocents. He began to think a lot...in ways he never had before. He decided he didn't hate these people after all. Maybe their leaders, but not the people, not even the average fighter. Surely most were like him - trained to hate, maybe now tired of the killing, praying for peace, but having little hope. This part of the world had such a horrific, stifling tradition. Tribes hating other tribes, religions hating other religions, sects within the same religion hating each other, nations hating nations. A homeland for the Palestinians even came to make sense to him, although he kept his own counsel on this explosive issue.

Though his views changed, he also realized the change would have no effect on his life or his job, or on anything that would matter. It was nothing but an intellectual exercise. Whether you fight because you hate or because it's necessary, you still fight. Whether they deserve a homeland or not, you fight to keep it from them because you know that the hatred and the leaders will never let it stop there. You fight because if you don't they will overrun you, and you can never let that happen, for no people have ever suffered so long, lost so much and struggled so hard for their land and their nation as yours have.

"I'll stop a little short here, Major, so you can go have a look". The driver's voice startled Engen from his ruminations. Grabbing the field glasses, he stepped out of the jeep.

"Five minutes to go", came the whisper from the front of the raft. Kabril checked his gear. Grenades, Uzi, knife, the bag of plastic explosives that can level a house or small building. His senses came quickly to full speed, as they always did when the time was near. Every sight, sound, smell and movement registered, and he assessed them all, instantaneously, with a fierce intensity. Every fiber in his body, every synapse in his brain was at full alert. He never felt more alive than at these times. Now his heart pounded in his chest.

They were out of the boat into knee-deep water, then running low, carrying the raft as they headed for the shadowy dark of the rocks across fifty meters of sand at what was low tide. The darkness was pitch black with no moon, but Kabril's eyes had adjusted and he scanned the ridge above them as they moved. He caught a glimpse of motion a millisecond before the world exploded in white light and deafening noise. The boat was ripped from his hand and he dove as far as he ever had toward the rocks.

Conflict, violence, pain, suffering...all from a difference of perspective on the same issue. But it's not different, or even similar creatures harming other creatures. It's the same species harming their own. So little doubt on either side, almost never a

9

nod to what should obviously be the logical position, or conclusion. I, Luggalor.

1995

DETROIT, MICHIGAN

With winter just ahead, and a few days of days of clear, pleasant, crisp weather, it seemed all of the city was intent on being outside. A sharp, fresh light the planet offers in early morning shone on people strolling through the park on their way to work. Steam rose from the cups of those with enough time to sit on a bench and read the morning paper, while others rubbed their hands together and tilted their faces to the sun to ease the chill from a long night outside. Runners circled the lake while cyclists flashed by, accompanied by the distant sounds of streets and buildings coming to life.

As the light rounded toward mid-morning, mothers and toddlers, some in pairs, some alone, most with strollers, began to gather for their ritual. Blankets were spread, children were hoisted, talk was light and pleasant. Carts, filled with sausages and hot dogs, large twisted pretzels, skewers of meat, appeared with their owners to join the lone early entrepreneur who caught the first or second cup of coffee crowd.

Only a few streets over the men languishing on street corners looked as if they had always been there. Overnight, through the summer, the fall. Leaning against the battered storefronts, or a bent pole with its mangled street sign. Crouched on their haunches on doorsteps. Blank stares, some glares. No movement.

Around a building's corner in a small alley, the early enterprise of the streets heated up. From both buyer and seller, cigarette smoke curled into the still air. Money was exchanged. Small parcels were pocketed.

The diversity of the streets and parks, of lifestyles and means, or lack of means, is stunning. All from this one species, with so little diversity in their genetic code...essentially identical. I, Luggalor.

"Our primary objectives for the next twelve months must be to somehow show a profit, increase earnings, and get our lenders back on our side. It is essential that every decision we make reflect a commitment to these priorities. I don't need to remind you that there are two issues facing us that could seriously undermine our efforts."

Dear God, is this guy a Neanderthal...or maybe this is still the modern corporate man... likely and infinitely more frightening. Sam Bradley was chomping at the proverbial bit to take Robert Quigley on, but he knew if he did it in this meeting it would have to be with more subtlety than he would like.

"The union contract is coming up and their main focus on extended employment security is one we cannot budge on."

Christ, where do they teach these guys to talk. Sam studied his adversary. Smooth, clear, pale complexion, dark hair close-cropped but with just the right hint of fullness, tortoise shell glasses, standard issue boardroom blue suit, starched white shirt, links, red and blue rep tie....everything about this guy is standard issue...a clone of the models for Brooks Brothers in GQ. Except his jaw isn't quite that prominent. Yeah, that's it...weak chin. Maybe he'll fold under attack. Sam chuckled to himself, wondering if the Eastern Europeans had any idea what they were in for. Would all their emerging capitalists and captains of industry evolve into Robert look-alikes and practice the screw-everyone-but-my-boss-and-the-stockholders philosophy for a successful life?

"And even more important than our resolve on the extended security issue is the effort we're going to have to put forth to get around the new emission standards. The good guys obviously overplayed their hand trying to dismantle excess regulation and fight the Greens. And now we have to deal with the backlash.

They will ruin us. It could mean finally having to go through the monumental retooling and restructuring necessary to accommodate significant numbers of highly fuel efficient, even electric cars. We all know the devastating effect that would have."

Sam couldn't wait any longer. "Robert, don't you think it might be wise if we try to remember what happened to this industry the last time it ignored the writing on the wall from the oil barons and objective, reasonable scientists...the last time it didn't adhere to the pulse and wishes of educated people and their few honorable representatives, the last time it didn't respond to the mood to clean up the air and develop more energy efficient products. When it let the almighty short-term bottom line override the collective intellect and infinite wisdom of those visionaries who uttered strong warnings...you do remember what happened, don't you? The Japanese sent small cars a human could parallel park, cars that didn't use much gas, and our people liked them so much they made like rabbits and for a while there were two in every garage. It precipitated the good ole U.S. auto industry losing its lead...maybe forever."

Darkness, no images, none of Sam's thoughts were there for me. Only the words. It was sudden and I was confused. The lens... something was wrong with the lens. I felt relief as I remembered the duplicate. Maybe this had been the Council's intent all along, not the uncharacteristic duplication and waste of producing two just because the humans have two sight mechanisms and I might have needed them both at once. I had known from the beginning there was no chance of that, that their thoughts and mental images come from the interrelationship of their two sight mechanisms and other senses. And why had not the Council already provided me with the duplicate, so I would not have to...worthless rumination, waste of time. I had to attend to the problem and restore the images and thoughts.

The message traveled intergalactically, across eons of light years, instantaneously. The replacement, coded "Luggalor", arrived back just as quickly, with a message that the problem was being analyzed. *I had access to all their thoughts once again.* I, Luggalor.

Robert felt the heat glow on his face, his anger and rage were at full cry as soon as Sam had uttered his initial mocking question. A goddamn liberal...what a contradiction...a liberal on a corporate board where everyone should at least agree on the rudimentary principle that in a free market system, everything will be taken care of due to the forces and dynamics of the market...without intervention. Maybe this guy is our token. I've been warned but I didn't expect him to be this bad.

Again, everything went blank. Nothing but words. I was incredulous. They were becoming quite sloppy. Two mistakes in the same millennium...quite uncharacteristic indeed. But this was interesting, some real mental hostilities here. I was more eloquent and urgent with my next request. I, Luggalor.

The message was sent, a correction made, and I was again wired into the thoughts of each individual in the room. I, Luggalor.

".... out of work employees will be rehired as the market dictates. There will be excellent career change opportunities in many cases. Sure there will be some casualties, but it's nothing personal...just the way the system operates. You know that," Robert said, finishing a quick defense of the market's dynamics.

"Sam, I, nor I imagine anyone else in this room has forgotten what you are alluding to. But certainly I don't need to remind you that if our profits drop because of the contract or the new standards we will have to put additional people out of work and our very existence could come into question. We can better contribute to eradicating environmental problems and providing jobs if we are a strong, profitable company." Peter Reisling quickly took the conversation, and Robert knew it was to defuse the discernible tension now in the room. Peter was the President and Robert's boss, and Robert was convinced he knew Peter very well. He had studied his every word and action from the day he was promoted to

Executive Vice President, as he had always done with every person he had worked under. He knew Peter would approve of his reply to Sam's accusations, and inject very subtle praise for his views that would further raise his stock with the other board members... card carrying, conservative, free-market capitalists all. Ten years at the outside. He was sure he would have Peter's job within ten years.

Sam knew the time was not right to continue his attack, that the others would grow impatient with him if he did. Peter had shifted the focus to the current figures and the meeting would now remain geared to creating and maintaining a rose-colored short term. But Sam was upset, cranky, combative. He couldn't let it pass, and as he began to speak he felt justified about continuing - these people needed someone to tell them. It was his duty. "Look, I don't mean to belabor the point but we've got to establish a long-term policy to handle these two issues so that in the years to come our employees will be content and productive, the company will have sustainable profits and be able to grow, and the environment will be on the mend. The two major problems in the U.S. business community are greed and more greed. We've got merger and acquisition gurus creating enormous fees and wealth from nothing while they take apart viable businesses, and corporations like ours sacrificing the future for the holy grail of next quarter's bottom line. We've got to stop creating money from illusions and terminal products and start creating quality services and goods with integrity and a future. And we've got to take care of our people and the environment. Certain companies, and nations, have proved it works." He paused for a moment to gage expressions, then continued. "The irony is, if we research, develop and retool quickly enough, for electric or hybrid vehicles, it should lead to a dominating, highly profitable position in the evolution of our industry. The search for alternative energy and fuel sources is inevitable, with or without us."

Sam looked around the room. Maybe one, if he was lucky, 'sort of' sympathetic ear. He wondered if nine to one is about

15

average on similar boards...the 'ayes' have it...more greed, more denial, more short sightedness...ahead full throttle. It wasn't as if he was professing a socialist state. He'd made his share of money in the corporate world, and enjoyed the rewards of his success, but the business environment was changing, and whether it's because of a dedication to a policy of long term, consistent growth for the company or the improvement of the lot of mankind and the environment...everyone had damn sure better be ready to keep up.

1995

Northwest Territories

"Father, is Li, the man who was here to buy the skins, really a reporter?" Did he really come here to spy on you and get you in trouble?"

Hinte stared at his son, the fire in his eyes as bright as the ten-year old boy had ever seen it. The vein on the side of his neck was huge, bulging, as it always was when he was angry. "Don't ever mention that name again in this house. Don't ever let me hear you speak of it to anyone." The words were measured, spoken quietly, but with a raw edge that carried a crushing force. Hinte suddenly stood and left the table, his coffee untouched.

"Mother, is what Father does wrong? Should we not kill the baby seals?"

"Come, sit by me," she said, as she pulled her child close, resting his head on her shoulder, her fingers stroking his dark, thick hair. "My parents, your great grandparents, and generations of our people before them have been hunting and fishing to provide for their families, to create the community we live in."

Kotah was comforted, as he always was, by the soft, song-like sounds of his mother's voice. Everything she said, everything she talked about, was always spoken of in the same manner...like her stories of the magic places.

"We are good, gentle people. We wish no one harm, only comfort in life. But because of where our ancestors settled, the water and the fish and animals were the only way to provide for the families. It is the natural way of God. Everywhere on this earth, from the beginning, man and animals have taken other animals for food, or clothing and shelter, or to trade and sell. If you think of the killing of one small creature, helpless to defend itself, you lose your sense of what is right and wrong, your true understanding of the natural ways of God's world. You do not see how everything fits together, how something dies so something else may live, how it happens millions and millions of times every minute, in every river and ocean, on the land and on the ice, in all the places where there are great forests and deserts. How a life ends, others are preserved, others begin. It is a never-ending cycle, like the light and dark, the sun and moon, the cold and warmth, the summer and winter. You must think of it like this. We are doing what God intended when he led us to this land...we are doing what our ancestors have done...we are doing what is right. And do you know what proves what I am telling you? We are happy and content. In other parts of the world, where the reporter Li lives, they kill many more animals for food and clothing than we do here. They raise animals for the sole purpose of eating their flesh and wearing their skins, not for protection against the cold, but for decoration. And they treat them cruelly, sometimes starving them before they kill them. They also kill people. There is much violence and unhappiness there. Once before, men came and made us stop taking the seals. We could no longer sell the skins because some countries passed laws against them. The ice has been rapidly melting, caused by the wasteful burning of fuel by the same societies who condemn our means of sustaining our families, making it even harder to replace the seals with other creatures we can barter or sell. Your father and the other men stopped taking them for some years, but our lives became hard, and there was unhappiness. When people came to buy them once again the men went back to what they could do to provide for the families. And happiness returned. No, Kotah, what your father does is not wrong. You must believe this in your heart. You will hear otherwise, but it is from people who do not understand our land, our lives, the natural way of God. You must always know the truth in your heart. You must create a safe place for it, and keep and protect it there."

1995

THE CARIBBEAN

The large parrot fish hovered, feeding off a yellow clump of brain coral, and its beautiful coloring of pastel greens and pinks reminded him of a recent trend in interior decorating. An array of small fish in brilliant shades of yellows and blues were scattered just beneath the huge purple filigree of fan coral, and then he noticed the school of squid on the bottom. Taking a breath, holding his mask, Robert lifted his fins out of the water, slid into a head down attitude, and kicked. In only fifteen feet of water, he was down in an instant. Falling in behind the creatures, he watched intently through his mask. Tiny, maybe four inches long, they were mesmerizing, with their eyes pointed backward toward him as they squirted forward in unison. Darting to the right, or left, or straight ahead, they always moved in a perfectly synchronized ballet. Staring until his lungs began to beg, he finally rose, cleared his snorkel, and continued to move along the surface. Approaching the large rocks off the shore of the island he saw a steep drop off, a wall. Twenty feet beneath the surface was a large school of angel fish, Sergeant Majors, each the size of his hand...hundreds of them, shimmering like dark blue satin, tightly packed together and moving through the water very slowly. Again he kicked down to have a closer look. It was the largest school of fish this size he had ever seen. *Incredible, absolutely incredible. What's the phrase?...living aquarium....something like that. I never tire of looking at these beautiful creatures in this amazing environment. Blows my mind every time I see it.* Again his lungs ached for air. Rising to the surface, he began the swim back to the boat.

Robert climbed the ladder onto to the transom and pulled off his mask and fins. Removing the onboard shower head, he rinsed off the salt water, then stood up to dry off. He felt wonderful. An early morning swim was one of his favorite things about a sailing trip in the Caribbean. Refreshing and good exercise after the usual bout of drinking the night before, and since the sun rises early in these latitudes, it was already at an angle that brilliantly illuminated the world beneath the surface. He stepped through the companionway, down the steps, and entered the warm glow of the teak and holly cabin.

"Good morning, Nelson. Did you sleep well?"

"Morning, Robert. Yes, I did. How about you?"

"Yes, very well, until about six o'clock. But that's normal for me down here. It seems I always wake up by six regardless of what time I go to bed or what I do the night before."

"Coffee?" Nelson asked.

"Yes, thank you. That's all right though, it gives me a chance to read, relax, swim, and the mornings are so glorious here. Liz still asleep?"

"Yeah, and probably will be. Said she wanted to sleep in."

Robert picked up the cellular telephone, dialed a series of numbers, then gave instructions that patched him through to a line in Washington. "Harold Carmichael, please. This is Robert Quigley." There were a few moments of silence before Robert heard the familiar voice. "Harold, what's happening with the mileage? Have you got the votes yet?"

"Harding and McMurtry are still holding out and I think that's all we need," was the reply from Harold.

"I think we contribute to them both. I'll give you a choice," says Robert. "Either tell them we'll drop our support or we'll increase it. We can get pretty much anything to them through their PAC's. Make it clear how important this is to us and to them. Harold, we've got to have those mileage standards modified or at the very least delayed. There is no alternative on this one. I'll call you again tomorrow so I can keep up with your progress. You've got my number down here if you need me any sooner. Ciao."

Robert picked up his book and coffee and climbed back on deck. He stretched out in the cockpit to read, across from Nelson, who had come out just ahead of him.

"You still trying to slow the cleansing of the earth by buying off politicians?" Nelson asked as he put his book in his lap. "You know acid rain has had a real effect on that gorgeous little trout stream of the club's where you and I had such great luck a couple of years ago."

Robert recognized the familiar clarion call to battle for the two old friends.

"Nelson, are you accusing me again of contributing unduly to the disintegration of the well-being and future of the human race and all of God's other creatures and plant life? What gives you the right to even hint at such a thing when members of your exalted profession are delaying an end to the incredible death and suffering brought on by AIDS, cancer and other horrible diseases because they are so greedy and egotistical they won't share their research. And what about those cattle ranches you own an interest in Brazil that I'll bet a dollar to a doughnut are sitting on what was once a piece of the great rain forests before they were slashed and burned and made to look like a set from Rawhide."

"It's undeniable there is some of that going on, and there are unprincipled doctors and scientists as well as unprincipled members of any profession, such as yours. It doesn't mean you or I have to act that way."

"Act what way?"

"Just a minute, give me a chance to finish. As for the answer to your second question, I'm checking into it. I'll sell my shares if it's true," Nelson stated with conviction.

"Act what way? Am I being unprincipled by trying to protect my company, the people who work there, and those stockholders who own it? By trying to maintain the capital to produce products that can compete in an increasingly competitive marketplace? Everyone wants to know why we don't seem to be as competitive anymore, but they usually forget that the competition doesn't have a government that regulates and restricts them like old Uncle Sam does. They forget that the only restrictions their governments issue are those that prohibit us from being able to trade in their building. Asian governments don't have an EPA to contend with. They attack parts of the environment like it was Pearl Harbor. We're not playing on a level field, Nelson."

"That's true, but it isn't going to make things any better if we all destroy the planet together. Each of us has got to show individual responsibility. We're all going to have to sacrifice for a while...it's the only way we have a chance. There were some questions for a time as to the actual ramifications and long term consequences of many of the so-called violations of the environment, but there is a consensus now. We're really screwing up, and if we don't stop the bill may be unpayable."

"Well, I'll tell you what I think about the consensus. In a lot of cases it's bullshit. Most of the EPA's holy crusades have less to do with protecting the environment than they do with getting self-righteous members of congress' votes by providing them a bandwagon to jump on for an attack on the pollutant or process that's the current media darling of the month. And, of course, saving jobs and promoting careers. What's a good environ-mentalist to do without plenty of environmental abuses to criticize."

"It still comes back to greed, Robert. Couldn't you survive if you allocated the funds necessary to meet the standards? Surely you realize that in the long run we'll all be better off. There shouldn't be a choice."

"There's nothing wrong with a little greed, Nelson. You know that. It fuels a market economy and you've probably noticed our system receiving some rather rave reviews around the world these days at the expense of some others. If the private sector is allowed to be profitable, research, development and philanthropy will flourish and solve many of the problems you want a terribly inefficient government to attempt to handle. Besides, it seems rather strange for you to be criticizing greed when you make enough money each year clearing arteries and sewing parts of pigs into people's chests to have saved the spotted owl on your own. A little less take-home and our health care system wouldn't be endangered."

"We had it your way for most of the eighties and into the nineties," Nelson said, "regulations in many areas were relaxed or done away with, great tax incentives, everything that should have been needed to create your fertile environment. And the economy flourished. You're right on the mark about how all that works. The trouble is, while the economy was flourishing and a lot of people were collecting fortunes, the number of homeless was soaring, the environment was getting worse, we became more dependent on importing oil, ended up hopelessly in debt, and drugs and violence have turned parts of this country into a virtual free-fire zone. Philanthropy, Robert? I think not. Try greed."

"All right, you guys, the world's problems will have to wait until you tell us whether you want an omelet or pancakes for breakfast. There's plenty of fresh pineapple, kiwi and sausages to go with either." Robert turned to look at the beautiful face of his wife Phyllis, smiling up from the cabin.

The lee rail was in the water and Robert braced himself with all his weight on his right foot as the graceful sloop charged upwind in the sparkling, late afternoon sun. He loved being at the helm on this point of sail, conscious of the beautiful power of the yacht charging through the waves while he strained to keep her flying ahead on a dead solid straight line.

"Can you flatten it out a little?" The cry came from down below. "We're trying to get the hors d'oeuvres together."

Women. Robert thought back to the morning's conversation. Nelson was his only close friend who was a certified liberal. Best friends since prep school, it seemed that time had hardened each of their political positions, but never appeared to have harmed their personal relationship. They continued to bait each other, and argue, and go after one another with vigor...yet even when the arguments became heated, they inevitably ended with laughter. It was that way because each respected the other's intelligence and opinions. If the truth were told, and of course it never was unless they were too drunk and accommodating to remember it, each of them had slightly more sympathy for the other's views than they would ever express.

Robert knew he came by his conservative bent in a traditional fashion, as his grandfather and father were true guardians of the faith. Of course, the terminology had become somewhat confused over the years, but the beliefs about federal intervention, regulations, and money being spent on what the private sector and local government should handle were still the foundation of the breed. The best government was the least government. He grew up around angry epithets hurled at even the slightest mention or reference to a federally-funded social program, or regulations, or guidelines. States rights was an often heard phrase, and even he, at a young age, wondered when his father said he admired some of the principals of George Wallace. Later he understood. A number of the kids he went to school with through Andover and Yale were from similar backgrounds and held similar views, and then he ended up at the Wharton School for a graduate degree and was introduced to some serious right wing market purists. Robert was convinced he had as much of a social conscience as most. He just didn't believe that the government should act as architect, administrator, and bank for every program that liberal, vote-seeking legislators deemed worthy of the taxpayer's money. If the market was provided a fertile environment, and left to prosper by its own devices and creativity, it would provide jobs and opportunity at the lower end for many people now dependent on government handouts, and wealth at the upper end to fund charitable programs for those who for some good reason could not take advantage of the opportunities. Corporations would have profits for research into reasonable technologies that could address environmental problems that are real...not fabricated. There would be money to fund medical research and the arts, and assist the elderly and the infirm...all the things the government tries to handle and never handles efficiently. There was no doubt in his mind that the American sense of philanthropy, coupled with impetus from strategically placed tax incentives, would accomplish far more for the huddled masses and the planet than the government ever would...or could. But businesses have to be able to operate with few restrictions in order to flourish...and be able to provide all this. And as for those with no good reason, who won't take advantage of an opportunity when it is offered to them...screw em!

Robert glanced at Nelson and saw he was engrossed in his book. "Phyllis, could you hand me a beer, please?" He took a long pull on the ice-cold Heineken and spoke in the most serious tone he could muster. "Nelson, what do liberals think now about closing down our nuclear power plants, which forces us to rely more heavily on imported oil, which forces us to put thousands of sailors in the imminent danger of close proximity to the nuclear reactors on their ships while they're steaming toward the even greater danger of a war to protect the oil we wouldn't need so much of if we had not closed and stopped developing nuclear plants?"

2000

CHARLESTON, SOUTH CAROLINA

John Champion was in the pose. Hands stuffed in the rear pockets of his jeans, palms in, feet apart, weight shifting slowly from side to side, chest expanded, head tilted slightly back so he could flex his neck...and make it look huge. His head turned slightly from side to side, eyes darting, looking his cool, tough-guy best while trying to keep anyone from noticing how often his eyes locked on Shawn's legs. Perfect, muscular thighs and calves tapering to thin ankles, tan from the summer, not ten feet in front of him, exposed to his view in her short cheerleader skirt. Not quite as good looking as Linda, he thought, but close, and definitely the best body in the whole school. The light from the bonfire cast a soft, flickering glow on the incredible legs. He imagined her beautiful bottom, white and firm above the brown legs, with the tiny, fine, silken wisps of hairs. He thought of Friday night...his fingers caressing... The familiar stirring was in his crotch, the cloud was forming in his brain. He had been staring too long, knew he must quickly think of something else. The game tomorrow night. He tried to visualize catching his first pass. Told himself to listen to what Coach was saying. Thought of algebra problems. Picked out faces in the crowd. It eased.

John felt proud, standing there with the team. All the other kids envied him. He loved the pep rallies, especially the first one of the season. *You stand in front of all these people like a gladiator, or a god, and you listen as the coaches and teachers and cheerleaders say great things about you...and then they cheer for you....again and again.* The band broke into the fight song. His chest again swelled, he flexed, and the width of his neck approached the width of his head.

Jesus, think about the end of the game... last play...winning... stretched out... ball on my fingertips in the end zone. His eyes were locked on the legs again and it was back, worse than before. *Christ, why'd I wear the tight jeans?* He looked wide to the left and right, desperately trying to make it go away. He spotted Horace standing off to the side, with Ricky, Ervin, Andy and a boy and girl he didn't know. *Horace is all right. Came out for the team last year, tough and pretty fast. But he's small and didn't know much about the game.* He thought of last year's banquet and Horace walking to the podium to get his letter. The sports jacket with the wide padded shoulders was too big, as was the shirt collar that wasn't meant for the bright paisley tie. Coach Blackwell handed him the letter and shook his hand. His mother sat with her head cocked, very erect, and looked so proud. But she didn't look comfortable. *She's young, but seemed older with the heavy makeup and slicked-back hair.* That was the first time he had seen anyone from Horace's family at a school event or game. He remembered wondering if she felt out of place with her tight skirt and low cut blouse. *Coach should have given Horace more of a chance, worked with him more. He could have improved, played more and maybe he would have come out again this year. Ricky and Andy are the wrong group to hang with. They do drugs pretty heavy, deal some, carry blades, are terrible students. I hate to see Horace running with them.*

His ruminations had eased his problem, but then Shawn bent forward for the beginning of a cheer, legs apart and straight, hands held just above the ground and twisting back and forth. John watched the black panties stretch tight, exposing a glimpse of the bottom of her cheeks. Again he felt the heat, the fog, the pressure. He didn't even try to look away.

"And now a word from this year's captain, John Champion."

Holy shit.

Stepping forward, he tried to look cool....was sure he didn't... knew there was a visible bulge in his jeans.

His father spoke as the last mouthful of egg-soaked toast disappeared into John's mouth. "The test scores for the school are way below the national average again, even dropped some from last year."

"Well, dear, it's certainly not our children who are bringing them down." There was a warm smile from their mother for John and his sister. "We all know what the problem is. The blacks and the Latins just don't have the same skills, or maybe it's motivation. I don't know, but I do know that's what brings the averages down. I've even heard it from the teachers, although I couldn't possibly say who."

Are they prejudiced? John wondered. He had even wondered a few times if he was.. *They never say nigger and never say anything about the black families in church. They didn't say anything when I brought a few of the black guys from the team over that night to shoot pool, but they didn't look too happy. They never say anything that sounds all that prejudiced, but there's lots of little comments like those. I guess they aren't really prejudiced. Prejudiced people really hate blacks and think they're scum. They tell jokes about them, and I know enough of those people to know the difference.*

"I've got to go," his father said, "Jimmy Hartley's speaking at the Rotary breakfast this morning."

"Are you going to vote for him, Dad?" John asked.

"I sure am, son. He's the only candidate that's got the sense not to want to raise taxes and the guts to vote against all the increases and government programs, no matter what they're for."

Horace's mother unlocked the door and crept into the small apartment as quietly as she could, not wanting to wake any of her four children. Carefully, slowly pushing open the door to the bedroom, relief washed over her. Horace was asleep. It was one in the morning, she stepped out of her high heels, tiptoed into the living room, then slumped, exhausted, into the plaid, stained easy chair. She thought about the weekend, getting some rest, then her days. Up at 6:30 a.m., she awakened the kids at seven to be sure they had milk and cereal and got off to school. After nine hours at the bakery she went to Oscar's and served drinks, got felt up, and listened to bullshit until closing time.

Her thoughts turned back to Horace. *I'll do anything short of kill him to keep him from the gangs and drugs. It's gotten real bad real fast. There's always been worry in families like mine and trouble for kids to get into, but when I was growing up it was mostly stealin and fightin and drinkin. Sure, there was drugs, but it was just weed and some smack that only the junkies, whores and pimps used. But now there's crack and meth everywhere, people dealin, even the littlest ones are runners...nine, ten years old, and lots of guns. Kids dyin. Lots of kids dyin. I've got to keep my family clean.*

The fist crashed into his cheek and he felt pain, then numbness before the next blow caught him on the shoulder and sent him lurching backward, tripping over a shoe. The boot was about to explode against his ribs when he came awake, eyes wide and frantic. After the few seconds it took to be sure it was another dream, Horace felt the tension and fear slip from his body. Relaxed now, he was able to think clearly of the times his father had started with his mother, then turned on him since he was the oldest and biggest. But he was not the size of his father, or nearly as strong. When he tried to defend her, it had only been worse. Jumping out of bed, shaking his head to clear it, he kicked his brother awake on his way to the floor.

"What's a matter, baby, can't you sleep?" His mother was collapsed into the chair, limp as a doll, a cloud of cigarette smoke hanging in front of her face, as Horace walked into the tiny living room, rubbing his eyes.

Jennifer Stark-Baker heard the giggles and high pitched "what you meeeean" from the back of the room and didn't have to look to know who it was. Striding purposefully to Horace's desk, staring at him the whole time, she asked for the piece of folded notebook paper he was holding.

Horace looked up with his best, smooth, cool-under-pressure smirk, "No Mam, I don't think you wanna be seein this."

Jennifer slowly pulled the paper from his hand and unfolded it, never moving the focus of her eyes from his. The message was scrawled, there was a sign at the bottom, and she knew it was from Andy.

> What colr is the teachrs bush blond
> or black? Nise ass for a honky

She stared at Horace, then at Andy across the room. "If you would learn to spell, Andy, I might take this as a compliment."

She walked back to the front of the room, dropped the note in the trash can and resumed writing on the board. *Like a verse from the Old Testament compared to what I used to see in Chicago, and almost every day.* But she knew there was something just as unsettling about this one, maybe more so. The bell rang, the room emptied, and she was alone.

Jennifer sat at her desk in the stark quiet that rushes so suddenly into a classroom after the final period ends. She gazed out through the window and her mind drifted. She was beginning her second year teaching at Central High. Jeffrey had been transferred to Charleston to become the comptroller of The Huntington Companies, a paint manufacturer and distributor. She was reluctant to accept the move at first...didn't want to leave her job, but then she began to think of it as a new challenge. She had known from the day Jeffrey told her about it that it was too good a promotion for him to turn down. It was just a matter of the time it took to reprogram her thoughts to accept it, then look forward to it, and making it a challenge was the best way for her to do that.

Jennifer thrived on challenges. When she received her masters degree from The University of Chicago she headed straight for the city system and asked to be placed in one of the real problem schools, where most of the kids lived in the projects. A week after she and Jeffrey were married she taught her first class at Jarrod. She knew she could make a difference, would understand and could motivate, was bright and perceptive and energetic. She knew she could change lives.

And when she left she honestly felt that she had. But at the same time she knew the changes in those lives, and the number of lives changed, was not close to what she had expected, or hoped for. She had recognized her idealism, but not her innocence. It wasn't that she had been shocked or couldn't cope with the things she saw or had to deal with. She had read enough and asked enough questions to be aware. It was the sheer enormity of the problems and the conditions that caused them. There were so many broken families, so much abject poverty, crime, drugs, violence...utter hopelessness and resignation to failure, all born from the devastating self-image and insecurities associated with a childhood without love, caring, nurturing and dreams. Positive role models were almost nonexistent. The kids had no intellectual concept of promise. Their visions were as dark and narrow as if they were trapped in a cave. Lacking any sense of confidence they could compete in the mysteries of mainstream society, they competed in their own. And finding self assurance in this alternative, many of them competed successfully and rose quickly through the ranks.

It was a society with a highly structured organization and strict codes of conduct. There was room for anyone who showed no fear...only blind, unquestioning loyalty. Being tough let you in, moved you up, and gave you a self-image that said you were somebody, you were appreciated, that you fit...the same self-image that every human being on this planet desperately needs.

There were many levels of jobs and duties in their society. Lookouts and runners, street dealers and wholesalers. The crack houses had people who ran them and people who guarded them. There were the numbers kids, the prostitutes and the pimps. Turf to be protected, gangs to join, and battles to fight. There were the young kids to get started taking and then dealing, or dealing and then taking, and the mothers to hook who tried to stay clean. Johns and old ladies to rob. And there was always getting high.

Each job carried its own status, dress code, income...much like mainstream society. The difference was, in this one, the more you moved up, the better you became at what you did...the more you became a target, the better the chance you would die or kill. And if you didn't move up? If you didn't have enough courage or cunning, or hadn't become numb enough to the violence to take part? Just like any other society that doesn't take care of its less fortunate, its indigent...they sink to the bottom and are victimized by all those above them. They only use, and steal to use, until they are of no use to anyone, and then it's only a matter of time.

Jennifer thought of the kids who would make it out. There were many, and she had helped. It was just that there were so many more who wouldn't. And then she thought again of the violence and the weapons....*so many goddamn weapons.*

She left Jarrod depressed, but within a few days after they arrived in Charleston she was again looking forward to her new challenge. It would be a totally different experience, and she was determined to get the most out of it, and to give the best she could to the kids and the school. With her knowledge, skills and experience, she knew she could be a positive influence in this predominantly middle-class school and middle-size town. The rewards of her efforts might be more evident here than at Jarrod, and while she would never duck a tough challenge, she was excited about that.

"Jennifer, it's so nice to meet you. We're so glad to have you here at Central." That was the greeting it seemed everyone at the teacher's reception gave her, or at least it was the only one she could remember. Just behind the greetings, handshakes and an occasional stiff hug, she detected a coolness. But she had expected it. She was aware of eyes constantly on her, and had felt self-conscious when Bob Holder, the principal, put so much emphasis on her degree and experience in the "tough Chicago city school system" when he introduced her.

"Do you go by Jennifer or Jenny," Jan Bond asked as she approached her in the parking lot after the reception.

"It really doesn't matter, but usually Jennifer," she said.

"I'm sure it will be nothing compared to your old school, but we are beginning to have our problems here, you know."

Jan was the youngest of the faculty members at twenty six, taught ninth grade English, and quickly became Jennifer's closest friend at Central. Jan's dedication to the job and her perception and intuition in her dealings with students and the staff had impressed Jennifer. *Most of the others are dedicated, but many haven't developed the ability to think freely and the vision necessary to handle the problems and diverse needs and abilities of the kids. They are too rigid, traditional, provincial, and, in some cases, prejudiced. Maybe it's their lack of worldliness, their upbringing, their education. Sure, they could be better trained, observe other systems, attend more workshops, and it would help. But that isn't the only answer. More money, leadership and dedication from the government and the systems are crucial. Teaching must attract the best, most capable people we have. It has to be a profession that offers the rewards and prestige of being an attorney, an architect, an accountant. Are any of these jobs more important? Certainly not now when we are in danger of losing a generation and our edge in many areas of scientific and commercial development is slipping. Education is the start to the answers to all of our problems. And only with the right emphasis and dedication to its hope and promise will you attract the caliber of people needed to fulfill that promise.*

Jennifer got up and walked down the hall to Jan's room.

"Hi. Tell me about Horace Wilson. He was in your homeroom last year, wasn't he?"

"Yeah, and I had him in English too."

Horace crossed the street to the corner of Alcorn and Waters and stopped in front of Nathan's grocery. Angel's Style Salon was next door. He knew this was their corner now, their turf. *Ice set it all up, told Andy and Ricky they had enough experience dealin' bags to have their own corner, to go big time. Said they'd need two lookouts who could also run until their business grew and then they could expand and add runners. Ice OK'd me and Ervin when we met him at the pep rally.*

Horace was nervous…real nervous…but excited. He felt the cold steel of the .25 automatic Ice gave him on credit…until he could pay for it from his take. Ice said he had to have it, had to be tough enough to use it if he was going to operate at this level. Horace remembered his words. 'This is serious shit, man, serious money you're gonna be workin and other gangs might try to move on you." Horace walked past Angel's to set up his post on the next block. He was wearing his colors, carrying a piece, getting ready to do it. Be the man…have money, clothes, cars…a tough chick just like Ice. Ducking into an alley he quickly lit the crack pipe. He inhaled deeply, and shuddered slightly with the rush. Stepping back out onto the sidewalk, he leaned against the brick wall, looked toward the corner where Ice would make the drop. He was wired. Never felt better.

Jennifer was lying in the dark with Jeffrey asleep next to her, thinking about what Jan said about Horace. "A pretty nice kid for most of the year. Kinda quiet, shy, not a good student, but not as bad as some. He never was any real trouble until he started hanging around with Andy and that crew. Rumor has it Andy's a dealer. In any case they're as bad as we've got here. Up until the Spring he was all right. Played on the football team, most of the kids seemed to like him OK, but he didn't seem to really fit in anywhere. His mother is a single parent, works two jobs. She seems to really care, but just doesn't have any time for him. When he started hanging around with those guys he seemed to be more confident, more self-assured right away. Trouble was, his new sense of self-confidence came out as the tough guy, rebel act. He started talking more jive, stopped interacting with anyone but that group. He picked up that crazy walk, or shuffle, that the black bad-asses all have. Became a problem in class...sarcastic, sulking, a chip on his shoulder. Stopped doing his work for a while, but after I told his mother, he was turning in his assignments again, but flunking most of his tests. The only reason he was promoted was because of what he had done the first part of the year."

The fog of depression seeped in, and Jennifer wondered why. She had seen so much of this before, and so much worse. *At Jarrod it seemed like five out of ten students had serious problems, and drugs were usually a major player. Here it's probably one in thirty. But maybe that's it. The influence isn't as great, the situation shouldn't seem as desperate, and yet it's still beginning to happen. And will probably get worse. Drugs are this generation of poor children's black death, and crack spreads the plague like a wildfire.* She decided she would have a talk with Horace the next day.

Horace watched as the silver Jaguar eased by him and on to the corner where Andy and Ricky were standing. It pulled to a stop. For a moment nothing moved. Then the driver's side door opened and Ice stepped out. He spoke across the top of the car to Andy, got back in, moved the car around the turn, then slowly down the other block toward where Ervin was. Andy looked around slowly, his eyes resting on Horace for a moment. Then he and Ricky turned and disappeared around the corner, following the direction of the Jaguar. His body tensing, Horace felt a chill run through his gut. The cockiness, courage, the sense of invincibility that the crack had given him was not strong enough to overcome his sense of alarm. *Why the hell'd they leave? Where'd they go?* He desperately wanted to go see what was going on, but knew he wasn't supposed to leave his post. He waited. Nothing. *What if they don't trust me, don't think I'm tough enough? What if Ice is telling Andy to get someone else? What if Ice knows there's going to be trouble and they're leaving me out here to get hit?* He lit a cigarette, inhaled deeply. Horace thought about running across the street, and home. *Come on, man, somethin happen. Where the hell are you? You didn say nothin about this.*

Looking up, he saw Andy back on the corner.

"Yo." Trying to sound tough, nonchalant, he shrugged his shoulders and gestured with the open palms of his hands. He wanted to show his irritation at being left out of whatever was going on, but knew he needed to stay cool. Andy motioned him to the corner.

"What's goin down, man? Where'd you go?"

"Ice didn wanna pass the stuff here on the corner. We went down the street where we weren't so out in the open."

"How come? Does he think there's gonna' to be trouble?"

"Naw, man, relax. He don't like to make deliveries and pickups right on the corner where we'll be doin business. Relax, man."

"I'm fine, man. I was just wonderin what the hell was goin down. You didn say nothin about leavin the corner and when Ice left, I was just wonderin." Horace felt his fear subside, *Everything's cool. Damn, shouldn have got uptight like that.*

"Go on back down the street, man, we're gonna' be doin some business real soon. We gotta have protection."

Horace walked back past Angel's. He wanted another blow

but didn't want Andy and Ricky to see him and think he was shook. Hands stuffed in his pockets, head down, trying to decide whether to reach for the pipe, he looked up and caught a glimpse of a car barely moving toward him, the oversized, chrome rims turning so slowly the pattern of the spokes was visible. Two cold, glaring faces stared into his eyes as it passed. His breath caught in his throat....the vice of instant, overwhelming fear squeezed his chest. Quickly casting his eyes down, he kept walking, faster. He heard a door open...but didn't turn.

"Horace, Christ, Jesus" Andy screamed, and then Horace heard the sharp crack of the shot.

Turning now, he stared for an instant at the barrel of the gun pointed at him, then dove for the doorway. He flinched at the next shots and the ricochet off the brick.

Andy screamed again. "I'm hit, help me."

"Waste him," boomed a deep voice he didn't recognize.

Pressing his back tight into the corner, he jerked the gun from his waist and released the safety. The instant he saw movement he stepped out and to the side, pushed the gun in front with both hands, and pulled the trigger as fast as he could, again and again. Explosions, screams. His eyes shut, he kept firing, and then he was running as fast as he could. Waiting for the pain. *Not hit yet.*

Jennifer had her plan, was ready to confront Horace. She had plenty of experience talking to kids in trouble, and figured many of them had been a lot farther gone than he was. He had a mother who cared about him, probably some values, and Jennifer was confident no one was any better than she was at getting right in a student's face and making them understand...challenging them. She was anxious, but confident. This was the true test of what she was about as a teacher.

Horace was one of the first students to arrive in homeroom,

which seemed odd to Jennifer, as he was usually late or right on the bell. She walked to his desk. "I'd like to see you after school today. Please wait here after sixth period."

The expression on his face...the wild, terrified eyes, shocked her.

"What for, Mrs. Baker. What's wrong?"

"Nothing, Horace, I just want to talk to you."

The announcements had come over the P.A. and the pledge of allegiance was at "one nation under God" when Jennifer noticed Bob Holder, the school's principal, standing in the hallway outside her door, motioning for her. She waited until the pledge was completed, then walked through the door. There were two men she didn't recognize standing next to Bob, and then she saw the two policemen in back of them.

"Jennifer, there's been some trouble. This is Detective Massey and Captain Smith. Is Horace Wilson in there?"

"What kind of trouble?"

"We think Horace Wilson killed a boy last night," Massey said in a deep drawl. "Probably a drug deal. We've got to go in and get him and he might be armed. Can you let the rest of the kids go and talk to him until we can get to him?"

The detective's words paralyzed her for a moment. But for only a moment, then she saw the pistol in Massey's hand and the handcuffs in Smith's.

"You are not going into my classroom with that gun. You can be goddamned sure of that. I'll bring Horace out here, but first you better tell me a little more about this because I don't for one second believe you."

Shock showed on the men's faces at her reaction. But they also recovered quickly. Smith's voice was hard. "Look, mam, we've got a dangerous situation here. We're going in to get him and we'd like you to cooperate. It would be the best thing for everyone, but we're going in one way or the other. We've got an eye-witness that says it was him."

"Wait here," she said.

Jennifer walked into the classroom, trying to steady herself. She went to the board and scrawled "don't forget the assembly at noon" to divert their attention and give her mind an extra few seconds to work. She looked up at the large, round clock above the board...8:25. *Time for the bell.* The minute hand perfectly bisected the 5 and its dot. *Ring now, God, please.* She waited. She wanted to look into the hall but knew she shouldn't, and realized she must do something that very instant to keep them from coming in. The shrill clang sent a rush of relief over her, but she still moved quickly. Stepping to Horace's desk, she was keenly aware of how fast the room was emptying. Her eyes fixed on his as he braced his hands to rise. Once she was standing over him she spoke firmly, but with a reassuring softness, and slowly, to give the other kids more time to leave. "Horace, there are some men here to see you. Don't worry. Everything's going to be all right. I promise you everything will be all right. You must do exactly as I tell you. OK?"

Horace's eyes darted toward the door, then to the window, then back to Jennifer. A look of fear, then a look of pleading masked his face, then he started to cry. He stood slowly, Jennifer encircled his shoulders with her arm, felt him tremble, and led him toward the door.

The instant they entered the hall Massey, pistol out and pointing upward, pulled Horace from her, spun him around, and pinned him to the wall, the side of his face distorting as the detective pressed it hard against a metal locker.

Jennifer slammed her hands against Massey's shoulder, pushed with all her might and wedged her body between them. "Take it easy, goddamn you. He's not going to cause any trouble."

There was a momentary standoff between them, neither set of eyes willing to budge. Then Massey backed off. Smith snapped the cuffs around Horace's wrists and they moved him quickly down the hall and through the side door.

It was only then that Jennifer was aware of how many kids were in the hall, how quiet it was. Her icy glare darted from one group to another, quickly sending them on their way. Suddenly her knees were weak, and she slid slowly down the locker until she was sitting on the floor. Her head tilted back and stopped against the cold metal. She was conscious of her mind not wanting to focus, or clear, or think. An enormous crush of sorrow overtook her

The promise of so many of the human's young...so often wasted. Each of them desperately needs attention, someone to look up to, to feel appreciated, to feel they belong to a community. Often they choose the wrong community. And when one of the caring humans tries to help...tries very hard to help...it is too many times too late for the chances to be good. There has been too much neglect and too many bad decisions. I, Luggalor.

2000

HUALLAGA VALLEY, PERU

As he quickly stripped leaves from the shrubs, glistening sweat pooled on Bernardo's copper skin, forming droplets that hung from his nose and chin before falling to the ground. He had been bent over, moving from plant to plant, for ten hours, and his back, shoulders, neck and legs ached. His two sons and three daughters mirrored his movements in other parts of the field, but they were young, and he knew they did not get as sore as soon. Bernardo looked forward to quitting today more than most days. It was Saturday, and his family will not work on Sunday. They will go to church and rest. It was important that they get as many of the leaves as possible into the sun so they will have time to dry. Then they could be bundled Monday morning before the truck comes in the afternoon to pick them up. He is sure he will exceed his quota, and this made him feel good. Also, it had been three months since his youngest son was born, and tonight he can once again have his wife. Bernardo always looks forward to this after a long day of working so hard, and misses having her before and after she has the babies.

Bernardo, his children, wife and newest son filed into the small church along with the other campesinos. Many came up to look and smile at the baby cradled in his wife's arms. Bernardo beamed; he was proud of his family. They genuflected, slid into the pew and sat down. This was the first day for Father Cordoba, the new priest, and Bernardo was anxious to hear what he would say.

When the priest started talking about temptation, sin and the forgiveness of God, Bernardo's thoughts turned to Father Moldaro. *He disappeared without a word two weeks ago. The mayor and the director of the campesino's association said he was called to another parish for an emergency, but no one thinks the church had anything to do with his leaving Culera. Father Moldaro had begun to say it was evil to grow the coca leaves and poppy plants. He said they were like Satan, that they killed many people in our country, and in the United States. The association could have taken him away, or the Narcotraffikers. The association does not like anyone talking against the leaves and will give a campesino's land to someone else if he grows other crops. The Narcotraffikers come with guns if they hear of meetings to discuss planting fruits, and those who go against them disappear, or are found dead. Or maybe it was the guerrilla fighters --Sendero Luminosa. Two weeks ago they killed the district governor, mayor, and judge in Pureno while they made all the campesino's watch. Father Moldaro preached all the time against violence...maybe it was them. Why did he say the things he said anyway? I know nothing of America and the other priests say it is a man's sacred duty to care for his family. If I grow papaya and melons I will earn one thousand dollars in a year and my wife will have to ride the bus six hours to town and then usually no one will buy. There is too much fruit that grows wild here. And it will be very dangerous for me. When I grow the coca I will earn five thousand dollars each year, it is picked up in front of my house, and the Narcotraffikers give me extra money if I make my quota. They built the church and the school and the television antenna.*

Bernardo had hardly listened, and the new priest had now finished. But Bernardo was sure Father Cordoba had said that if he works hard and takes care of his family, and prays for the other campesinos and says his rosary and doesn't listen to Satan and doesn't sin, he will be saved and go to heaven.

As they approached the door of the church to leave, screams and cries suddenly sliced through the quiet, still morning. Bernardo raised his arm and told his wife and children to wait, then hurried outside to see what had happened. Skin-crawling, breath-stopping terror washed over him. On the lone, large tree in front of the church, hanging from the lowest limb, was a priest's white robe. Drenched in blood. From the bottom of the robe two legs dangled, one with a foot, the other with only a bloody stump. The top of the robe was empty.

After they had eaten and said their evening prayers, Bernardo's family went to bed. They would be up early the next morning to finish putting the leaves into bundles. He again had his wife, but it did not make him glad as it usually does. Even while he was inside her he thought of the robe.

The council had long ago made the necessary adjustments. I could now switch lens from one human to another, to another, back and forth, any number of times, any number of lenses, any number of humans, without any problem. All the thoughts and perceptions, so often distorted by the filters that form on each lens of each human, are transferred instantaneously, so that I have crystal clear access to it all. I, Luggalor.

Bernardo worked very hard the next morning preparing as many of the leaves as he could. His thoughts were focused on his work...except for the numerous times when the image of the hideous robe and Father Moldaro's bloody stump returned. The truck arrived and the bundles of leaves were loaded. *I decided to go to the lens of the driver as he started back down the rutted, dirt road.* I, Luggalor.

"Adios, Bernardo, mi amigo" the driver shouted, his head poking through the window and looking back

Carlo, the driver, had discovered during the long morning that his partner for the day, the guard, didn't like to talk."Do you ever go to the Caballeros Club? There are many beautiful senoritas there," said Carlo.

"I have been once. I do not like that kind of place."

Well, if he does not like to talk I will not make him, thought Carlo.

There was no further conversation in the flatbed truck, piled high with dried coca leaves, as it rumbled through the valley. Carlo's mind was curiously blank except for what it registered from the road as he drove, the guard's not even that active. I could not recall having used the lens of a human before that produced so little thought. After I was certain there would be no interesting, illuminating thought from Carlo, I decided to assume my natural form and rest. It had been a long time since I had been in my natural form.

There was a river, with a narrow, grassy bank rising from the water's edge that ended abruptly in a thick forest. I laid down in the grass, leaned against a stone, closed my single sight mechanism, and listened to the incredible cacophony of sounds coming from the multitude of insects, animals and birds around me, the wind's gentle rustling of the plants, vines and trees, and the water moving in the river. The aromas of the grass and wood, especially the sweet fragrances of the many blooms and blossoms, gave me great joy.

Opening my sight mechanism to see the wonderful things I heard and smelled, I found a long narrow creature with a flat head staring intently at me. I wondered what the beings of this planet think as they see me in my normal form. Many of them have two sight mechanisms, as the humans do, rather than only one. Most appear to be fairly solid body forms with somewhat rigid, structured shapes. Quite a contrast to my non-solid, non-rigid, structure that can flow, change, disappear, and reappear.

I vanished and reappeared on another stone, on the other side of the creature. The dark head and two large sight mechanisms did not turn. I went to the lens of the creature and there was only recognition of what its sight mechanisms absorbed, no conscience or unconscious reaction unless its senses detected some external change. Not in a thinking way as with humans, but rather as a process that I sensed always functions the same. There was no reasoning or consideration of choices, just a consciousness waiting for something to occur that could be reacted to. Again I appeared on the first stone. As the creature's sight mechanisms saw motion again, the head turned quickly, but only slightly, and again stared at me. Suddenly the mechanisms shifted and the creature began moving away, its long, sleek, black body a thing of beauty as it was propelled forward by an elegant swaying motion. I watched it disappear into the grass.

How marvelous this planet is, with its extraordinary diversity of living things, its stunning array of beautiful sights, sounds and smells. How uniquely constructed are the dominant species, the humans, with their abilities to reason, feel emotion, adapt and invent. There is such potential here for harmony among all life, but there is so much discord and violence that prevents it. I, Luggalor.

2000

PARIS, FRANCE

Huan excused himself, walked through the door of the Bateaux, and stood on the port side, leaning against the rail. This was his second trip at twilight on one of the large tour boats that cruise the Seine, and he was not about to miss the sight he knew was approaching. As they came alongside Ile de Cite the familiar shape of Notre Dame filled his view. The sky, brushed with cirrus and filmy mare's tails, had turned brilliant shades of red, purple and orange overlaying pastels of salmon, pink and blue. As the cathedral slipped by, the magical moment arrived when the mighty buttresses were silhouetted against the celestial canvas. It was as stunning, awe-inspiring, perhaps even more so, than he remembered it. *Could a heaven of anyone's imagination be more beautiful. I love this city. The beauty, the history, the art, the people, the excitement...everything about it. I should go back inside now to my dinner. No, I will stay until the boat turns back. It will not be long and this is too magnificent a sight to leave. They are my friends, they will understand.*

Thoughts of the months he had spent in Paris as a student filled Huan's mind. He did not have the time to do so much sight seeing then, although he took every opportunity he had. After completing his third year at Harvard, he was selected to participate in a summer program in economics at the Sorbonne. That first visit to the Crazy Horse...remembering the evening brought an inward smile. Like the buttresses of a majestic cathedral silhouetted at sunset, the women of Paris never disappointed him with their beauty. His manners completely deserted him that first time, and he stared. The smile crept onto his face, and broadened, as he recalled that he stared again, just as shamelessly, last night.

"Huan, is something wrong?" It was Jon.

"No, nothing at all. I love the sight of Notre Dame at this time of the day and didn't want to miss it. I was going to invite you to come with me, but you were so engaged in the conversation that I just slipped out."

"Your food has been on the table for some time now and I am sure it is cold," Jon said. "Mine was not very hot when they brought it. The taste is good but certainly nothing to compare with the dinner last night at La Tour D'Argent. I am sure that is the best meal I have ever had. But this boat is fantastic, with all of its lights and those along the banks."

Sliding past one of the many barges moored along the river's edge that serve as homes, the powerful spotlights from the Bateaux illuminated a couple sitting amidst geranium-laden flower boxes, drinks in hand, as if they were awaiting surgery in the garish candlepower of an operating room.

"What do you think, Jon? Do those people like the Bateaux Mouches and their lights?"

The answer came from the barge as the man and woman raised their glasses and smiled.

"Everyone in Paris is a little crazy, Huan, don't you think."

Huan stared at the shapes on the ceiling from his bed at the Hotel Concorde Lafayette later that night, unable to sleep. Glancing at the illuminated numbers on his bedside clock, he saw it was just past two a.m., got up and stepped to the window. Below him the city was still ablaze with light. His view was framed by the Arc d' Triomphe to his left and the Eiffel Tower to his right, brilliant in its gold glow against the black of the night sky.

Tomorrow will be an interesting day. The first day of these conferences always is. It is ostensibly being held to contribute to the eradication of industrial pollution, but the tone is set by the sponsoring countries, in this case France and the United States, and it's usually clear from the beginning how productive the discussions and proposals will be. If there is a great deal of posturing and preaching by the hosts and other industrialized nations, these affairs are essentially worthless. Except, of course, to the executives, politicians and scientists from those same nations who will reap the benefits of seeing their hypocritical, pious attitudes and statements in their country's media.

Huan's thoughts turned to his family, and how his selection to come to Paris was a normal progression in their history and tradition. Their evolution could be viewed as a microcosm of the participation in the world order of what were once strictly provincial societies. A fourth generation Malaysian, his family immigrated to that Asian melting pot after a tribal war in China. They escaped with some of their wealth, and assumed leadership roles in various levels of government and commerce almost from the beginning. Huan is the third member of his family to have been educated in the United States and Europe.

The problems are immense for everyone, to be sure, but the differences between the industrialized and emerging nations relevant to the issue of pollutants is a chasm, and must be recognized as such. Nations such as mine have as their primary obligation the feeding, clothing and housing of their people. The development of any profitable industries is the first priority in fulfilling this obligation. There is barely enough money for the first or second generation technology and equipment we must use; it is ludicrous to expect us to be able to purchase or develop the technology required to effectively control the emission of pollutants. Surely the bureaucrats, politicians and executives from the U.S. and the other powers must realize this. It is a starkly simple fact.

There are many leaders from other undeveloped countries who are as aware and concerned as I am about the danger to the planet of environmental abuses. And if it is a problem for the planet then it is, of course, a more immediate problem for our people since they live where the pollutants are highly concentrated. But is it better to have people go hungry and suffer all the disease, conflict, human misery and death that goes with poverty, or is it preferable to release carcinogens and other dangerous substances into the air and water that cause serious suffering, hardship, and more death in the future? The answer, of course, is to solve both these problems. I know this. But I also know we will need a great deal of help.

Huan took one last look at Paris at night and then walked back to his bed. This time sleep came easily.

Sitting in the hotel restaurant early the next morning, Huan was convinced he would never become comfortable with a five dollar cup of coffee. It is a habit he picked up as a student in the U.S. and has continued to hold onto, although he still enjoyed the more traditional cup of tea. The breakfast was excellent for a hotel restaurant, and then he remembered the old saying that you cannot have a bad meal in Paris. Then he thought of the dinner at the Moulin Rouge a couple of evenings ago. *Beautiful, incredibly beautiful women, great acrobats, hilarious ventriloquist...but definitely a mediocre meal.*

Delegations or representatives from over fifty nations filled the room. The chairs and desks, each with a microphone, were arranged in a crescent. Earpieces for translations hung on the back of each chair. Huan always thought of the United Nations when he was in a room set up like this. The decor of the hotel was even contemporary. He also always thought of the potential.

The conference started with the usual greetings and welcomes from the hosts and distinguished guests. Following were hours of statistical-laden reports from various research organizations whose job it is to document the wretched state of the world's environment. And it seemed to Huan as if they were doing their job well, for wretched it sounded. There were some isolated bright spots. Acid rain content had declined significantly in certain areas of...he certainly could have guessed...France, Great Britain, Germany and the U.S.

They finally came around to specifics, and the first area of discussion was the release of chlorine and PCB's into rivers and seas, primarily by the pulp and paper industries. Huan listened attentively. One of his uncles was involved in a large pulp mill outside Kuala Lumpur for a number of years, and he was very familiar with the problems of toxins released by the pulping process. The speaker, an American toxicologist, began to speak of a specific area of the Volga in Poland and its high levels of toxicity.

"This issue must be addressed and addressed now. We have known for years the danger of the release of PCB's and chlorine, and steps have been taken in the U.S. and other countries to eliminate this problem that is so damaging to people, marine life, and entire ecosystems."

As the speaker droned on, making anyone who condones in any way even the tiniest release of these chemicals sound like a reincarnation of Hitler, Huan decided that this man was well versed in toxicology but didn't know a damn thing about world economics, political, or social systems. He patiently waited until questions could be asked.

"Surely you must realize that those of us in developing countries have known for a long time the facts and dangers you have so eloquently described." Huan tried to keep his edge of sarcasm from appearing too obvious, but doubted he was succeeding.

"The problem is not so much with awareness or understanding, but rather economics. The developing nation's first obligation is to develop industries that will feed our people and contribute to what is at least a functioning economy. This is not an easy task. We are poor and do not have the means to purchase or develop the technology needed to eliminate these toxic by-products of the limited industries we have. Instead, we are forced to rely on outdated, often antiquated processes and equipment that we purchase from countries such as yours that have tired of using them to contaminate your own waters, kill and injure your own marine life and people. Your country is one of the greatest polluters on earth. Your paper mills still spew out huge amounts of dioxides, methanol, chloroform, toluene and chloride dioxide. If your own industry, which definitely has the financial resources and technology necessary, will not comply with reasonable guidelines, what gives you the right to expect ours to? We welcome your advice, but not your hypocrisy, and we need to hear constructive proposals that address real solutions, which again, are primarily economic."

After a long moment of complete silence, a number of delegates broke into applause. Huan felt the flush of still-pumping adrenaline as he sat down. When he finally reflected on something other than what he had just said, it occurred to him that he was glad the individual countries selected their own representatives for these meetings. If it were up to the hosts, he was quite sure he would not be on the invitation list for next year.

Highly developed, sophisticated minds in this group of humans. Much the same as with other humans attending other gatherings dealing with serious issues. But their thoughts are so at odds on critical issues, even though the physical properties of each mind appear essentially identical. Problematic. I, Luggalor.

2000

CHARLESTON, SOUTH CAROLINA

The living room was small, impeccably neat, everything in its own, special place. And there were scores of things - pictures, vases, figurines, paperweights, knickknacks of all types - all mementos of a lifetime of collecting and receiving, and each commemorating some special moment, or person, or place. They were everywhere - on tables, etageres, walls, the mantle. Above the Chippendale couch was a large painting, ornately framed, of the last supper. Under this prized possession sat Lila May Robertson.

Silver hair perfectly coifed, gold-rimmed glasses perched just below the sparkling green eyes on the broad face, bright yellow dress resplendent on her matronly figure, hands in her lap and feet demurely crossed, she waited and thought. *Plastic slipcovers are put away in the closet and the doilies are on the arms. Silver coffee service is out in the dining room, with cups, saucers, spoons, sugar, cream. There's at least twenty tea cakes out and more in the kitchen. Hard candy in the jars. I know everyone will agree with me...we just can't let the good ole fashion values and traditions of our church and community go by the wayside. Mama never would have stood for it, neither would Aunt Lessie May. They would have got to the bottom of it, and would have been proud of me for doing it. Things shouldn't have to change. The Bible's teachings are the same now as they were back then, and just as right. There's too many newfangled ideas, too much immoral behavior among young people that we must do something about. When we can...*

She stood up suddenly, walked to the pantry in the kitchen and returned with a box. *I'll put the Godiva chocolates Paul and*

Sandy brought us from Brussels on the coffee table. Maybe someone will ask me where they came from. She glanced at the clock on the mantle. In five minutes the members of the Ladies Missionary Guild from the First Baptist Church would begin to arrive.

"I do think we need to plan the bazaar early this year, don't y'all? I've had just scads of people come up to me and ask when it's going to be and if they can bring things. I just know it's going to be the best one we've ever had. That new lady whose husband is a teacher at the high school, well she told me she blows glass. Can you imagine how hard you must have to blow? I've never. I think her name is Christian. Sort of a funny name, particularly for a lady."

"Kristin, Evelyn, Kristin is her name." Lila May was quick to correct her.

"I think we need to finish up the quilt we're going to send to Ron and Janet Black before we do or plan anything else. They'll have spent their two years in New Guinea doing missionary work and be back before they get it if we don't hurry."

"You're right, Esther. Who hasn't finished their work on the quilt? You're the only one, Irene?"

"Well, I know June hasn't finished her section either, but of course she isn't here. My eyes are so bad, my goodness, I just can't do that detailed handwork any more without my big magnifying glass...Herbert calls it my cheater...and the bulb went out. But I'll promise you, Lila May, I'll get it fixed and I'll get finished by this weekend coming up and I'll get June to finish hers too."

"Let's have some coffee and tea cakes before we try to get too much accomplished," Lila May said as she stood and motioned for the ladies to go into the dining room. "And I've got something else I think we're going to want to spend some time talking about."

"Good gracious these are wonderful. Are you ever going to tell us your recipe for these tea cakes? Lila May, there just isn't anything I've ever had to compare to these."

"Evelyn, I'll be glad to tell you what's in them. Flour, sugar, shortnin, and eggs."

"What about the liquid, Lila May?"

"Well, maybe I'll tell you almost all the things in them."

"That's not fair, Lila May, and what about how much of each thing?" Evelyn asks.

"Well, maybe I better keep that a secret too. My Paul and Sandy keep telling me I could be rich if I'd start selling them. I just might do that some day. Let's go back and sit down in the living room. I've got some pretty interesting news."

The four ladies sat down, their coffee cups perched daintily on their laps. Silence. "This is the quietist I believe I've ever seen this group," Margaret said as she looked at the others in the room. Her eyes stopped on Lila May. "Well, tell us. You know there isn't a one of us can wait long to hear interesting news."

"Well, it seems that three of the black families in the church are taking yoga classes at the recreation center."

"Where on earth did you hear that?"

"Janice Myers' daughter takes gymnastics there and when she was picking her up yesterday she saw the Johnsons, the Cunninghams, and the Hogans standing around in their sweat clothes. She couldn't think of any class they could be taking there at the recreation center so she went to the office and asked her friend, Elaine Adams, who works there in the office, what class they were in and she said the yoga class."

"Well, if that don't beat all. Yogas kinda weird, aint it? That's what they do in Japan and China, don't they?"

"Weird, you can say that again. It's what the Hindu religion does. It's a form of devil worship. It's demonic."

"I don't know anything about Hindus. How do you know so much, Lila May?"

"My sister Mabel went to Bombay one time, it's a city in India you know, and she said the people walked around in a fog, like they were all possessed by devils. And all the people in India, of course, they're all Hindus."

"Oh, heavens, Lila May, you don't mean it"

"My Word"

"Why, if that don't beat all"

"Gracious Goodness"

"Are the people in Bombay black?"

"Yes", said Lila May, "but I think they're not quite like the blacks here."

"Well, all blacks are different than whites. We all know that. The Bible says so and it also says that we shouldn't mix. I think we all feel the same, don't we? We don't have anything against them, but we'd feel better if we didn't have to mix, wouldn't we?" Irene asked.

"Do y'all know anything about what you wear when you do yoga?" Evelyn's eyes twinkled with excitement as she spoke.

"Leotards or gym clothes, I suppose," replied Lila May.

"Well, I saw this book one time," Evelyn said. "You have to understand it was about massage and meditation and I would have never, ever looked if I had any idea. It was in the bookshelf where I take my Taffy, my cat, to have a bath and get groomed. It had a picture of this man sitting with his legs crossed, you know kinda like the Indians used to. I think it's the same way you sit for yoga and he was naked! I mean of course you couldn't see anything because he had his feet in front, crossed like, you know what I mean. Do you suppose they're doing their yoga naked?"

"Oh, Evelyn, not in the recreation center."

"Margaret, I'm sure no one is doing yoga in the recreation center naked. They could be getting together at their homes, though, I suppose."

"It just makes me sick to death to even think of such a thing."

"Lord have mercy."

"I think we need to talk about what we should do about this."

"What do you think, Lila May? If we say anything people will think we're prejudiced."

"This doesn't have anything to do with being prejudiced," Lila May said, "First Baptist is a fundamentalist church and we're dedicated to serving the good Lord and I think we have an obligation to put a stop to any kinds of practices that are against everything we believe in, and anything that has to do with devil worship and demons is sure against those things. Just think of the influence on our young people."

"You're right Lila May, we've got to do something."

"I agree. My Heavens, what a mess."

"I don't think we should make any kind of announcement or anything. I think we should just tell a few people, you know, that would be concerned, and we can see how they feel."

"I know how Lillian will feel when I tell her...whew, why she'll have a conniption."

"Lila May, do you think we should tell Pastor Morrison?"

"I do, I mean he should know what's going on," Margaret said.

Lila May was silent for a moment before she spoke. "He should know but I think we should see what other people think first. I mean we don't want him to think we're being too nosy or spying on people or anything. I think we should tell a few people at the pot luck supper tomorrow night and see what they think. It's lucky that tomorrow's Wednesday and we can tell people in person at the supper. It looks better than calling them on the phone."

"Gracious, what a mess."

"Lila May, where on earth did you get these? Godiva chocolates. They're the best in the world, aren't they. I mean all the movie stars and all eat them. I hate to even ask but could I try one?" Evelyn asked.

"Go ahead, all of you have some. My Paul and Sandy brought them to us from Brussels. They were just there, you know. Paul was at a conference and he took Sandy with him. They said it was just wonderful."

"John, do you know any of those boys involved in the shooting the other night? I heard a couple of them go to Central."

"Yeah, Dad. One of the guys that got killed was in one of my classes last year. And Horace Wilson, they arrested him, he played on the team last year. Pretty bad stuff. He was a nice guy."

"Nice guy. My god! What's happening to our town? And then we hear what we did last night at the church supper."

"What, Mom?"

"It seems some of the black families in the church may be secretly practicing devil worship. Why is it always the blacks? We didn't have these kinds of problems before. I'm worried for you. You've got to be very careful who you associate with. Anything can happen. We've got to do something."

John Champion wondered again about his parents, about prejudice, and about Horace Wilson.

"Come on, boy, get dressed. You remember that whuppin you got last time you made me late? I'll damn sure do it again if you ain't ready in five minutes. Can't none of us be late for this. Too important. The niggers give us a real good reason to march this time. Shooting up the town over drugs and devil worshippin. Even the big shot do gooders oughta be upset about devil worshippin in their own church. We're gonna' make the white folks in this town see what's happenin here."

Everett Milligan went to the closet and took the robe from the hangar and the hat from the shelf. "Sons of bitches." He wondered if he should carry the .357 magnum. He decided he would, but he'd leave it under the seat, in case he got arrested.

"Come on son," he said, "I might even let you march with us today. Would you like that?"

"Yes, sir."

"Hurry up, woman, damn you. Get the little one and let's go."

Everett felt the excitement building. Felt edgy. Putting his arm around Everett Junior's shoulder, they walked out and climbed into the truck. His wife and six month old daughter squeezed into the cab alongside them and they headed for the heart of the city.

"Everett, all right, we're gonna' have us a time today."

"Buddy, hey man," Everett shouted back.

"Hey, ya'll, ol Randy's bringin five guys from Hopewell. You better let the boy march, Ev, mine's gonna'. We need lots of folks today, show em our unity."

"He's a gonna', Biggun, he's a gonna'," Everett replied as he looked down at his eight year old son and smiled. The boy's face lit up with a grin, and he pressed tight against his father's side.

Everett felt good. He always did when he's with them. Everyone liked him. He knew he belonged here, maybe the only place he ever felt he really belonged, and he knew he was part of something important. Something that people looked up to, or hated, or feared...but he knew it was something important.

He put on the robe and hood knowing he would stand out, that people would look on him with respect. Tall anyway, they made him look huge. He knew because Buddy told him he looked huge when he wore them. And Everett was glad the robe hid his skinny, narrow body, and the hood covered his face - gaunt, craggy, with a long, thin, crooked nose. A face he never liked. There weren't many times any more that he could wear the robe and hat. He wished there were more. His Daddy, and his Granddaddy, had worn their robes and hats often. But times had changed. Mostly for the bad, thought Everett.

He remembered the times in school when the other kids made fun of him, how he would sometimes fight back, but would usually lose. He wished they could see him now. There was that one horrible day when he came home with a swollen lip and black eye from a fight and his daddy took him to the boy's house and made him fight again. He fought as hard as he could because he knew his daddy would beat him if he didn't win. He lost again, but his daddy didn't beat him...he just didn't speak to him for a week except for calling him a pussy. As soon as he could, he quit school and went to work at the auto parts store Mr. Hyde owned. Anything about cars interested him, and he became the tire department manager before he was twenty-five. His parents didn't seem to mind when he quit school. *Daddy always said all the learning I really needed I could get outside of school, and he sure taught me right about the niggers. Mama too. Now I'll teach little Ev. They're like animals...killin and rapin and takin drugs. But they're smart like foxes. They get lots of important white folks, folks that like communists and Jews too, to like them. They fool em so they can't see it's the niggers, and now the homos too, what's makin this country weak, why there's so much crime and famiies are fallin apart. It's the white man that God chose to be in his image and being homo is worse than stealing and cheating in his eyes. Gay Pride march in this town...just after the nigger kids shot up each other. We'll show em we won't put up with it. We got to take our country back. The Klan ain't nearly as big as before, but now we got the skinheads and the Ayrian Nation with us, and websites and blogs all over the internet have lots of smart folks that thinks like we do. More groups forming all the time. More than ever. Folks are fed up.*

Everett moved through the crowd of twenty or so men and boys, standing tall, straightening his back, holding his head high. Greeting each one, he shook hands, slapped backs, patted the younger boys on the head. He was proud. He was somebody to be reckoned with.

2000

RONDONIA, BRAZIL

Jorge gently laid his daughter onto the tattered mattress in the bed of the rusted truck and covered her with a blanket. Maria curled up beside her and encircled the small, slender body with her arms. Jorge quickly jumped into the cab, and while his five other children stood and watched, the wheels spun madly, spewing dirt and rocks, as they pulled away from the small, unpainted wood house and headed down the heavily rutted path. He drove the old truck as fast as he could and its wild, bouncing dash enveloped it in a cloud of dust as Maria banged on the back window and motioned for him to slow down. When he reached the paved road he turned to the right, again slammed the accelerator pedal to the floor, and they slowly picked up speed until the heavy shaking of the steering wheel warned him he should go no faster. He was on B.R. 364, headed north towards Porto Velho.

The hospital waiting room was filled. Babies cried, old people slept, and most everyone else fanned themselves against the heat. Jorge tried desperately to find someone who would look at Gabriella. He knew she was very sick and they could not wait their turn. After the first few nurses he pleaded with ignored him, he picked up his daughter and quickly dashed through the large double doors. A doctor standing in the hall turned and asked, "What are you doing in here, Senor?" his eyes and voice at first hard with aggravation, but softening immediately when his eyes fell on Gabriella. "I need a cart here, quickly," he said, in a commanding tone, to no one in particular.

A nurse arrived pushing a gurney, they laid the child on it, and then they all disappeared quickly around the corner.

Jorge and Maria waited throughout the afternoon and into the night, speaking hardly at all. Everyone in the room seemed to be moving very slowly, as if they were sick. The same blank stares covered each of their faces, and Jorge wondered if these people would give him and Maria their diseases...if he might die soon after they left. This was the first time Jorge had ever been in a hospital, and he felt very uncomfortable. He wondered what they were doing to Gabriella, why they had not come to tell them what is wrong with her. Each time he stopped a nurse and asked, they either ignored him or told him to sit and wait, that someone would call him when they needed him or had information.

The nudge on his shoulder awakened him. Sitting up straight in his chair, he looked into the eyes of the same doctor who had taken Gabriella from him. He motioned for Jorge to follow him. They walked through the doors leading to the wards, and as soon as they were in the hallway the doctor stopped and turned to him.

"I am Doctor Malanga. Your daughter has Malaria and she is very ill."

Jorge felt his heart pound in his chest. He tried to speak, but his mouth was dry, and words would not come.

The doctor continued. "When your daughter arrived here she was near death. She may still die, but she is stable now and has been breathing somewhat easier this morning."

Again Jorge wanted to speak but he was not sure what to say. Only fully understanding the words "near death", he stammered, "Whhhen will you know if she will live?"

"It may be some time. You should go and get some sleep if you can and then come back. You can not see you daughter now anyway. We will do everything we can for her."

Jorge nodded and watched the doctor's face blur as his eyes began to fill. "Please try to make her well."

"Yes, we will do everything we can. I promise you. Now, I must ask you some questions and then you must give the nurse at the desk down the hall some information. Where do you live?"

"To the south, off BR364, about twenty kilometers from Ariquemes."

"Did you burn and clear the forest? Are you a farmer?"

"Yes."

"How many other people are in your family besides yourself and your daughter?"

"My wife Maria and our three sons and two other daughters."

"Is anyone else in your family ill now? Does anyone else act like Gabriella did when she first became ill?"

"No."

"You must bring your other children and your wife into the hospital so we can give them medicine to keep them from also getting Malaria. It is a very dangerous disease and it is common for people who burn and clear the forest to become ill with it. There are many mosquitoes and animals where you live that carry the disease and can give it to you. Is your wife here?"

"Yes. She is out there."

"Go get her and then go down this hall to the desk and give the nurse the information she asks you for. Then go try to get some sleep and come back. When you come back you may come to the desk and ask for me. And pray for your daughter." *Another poor campesino, left the slums for his dreams in the forest. Doesn't realize the soil won't support crops for any period of time, that he'll have to move again, and again. So many thousands of acres of one of nature's and the environment's most precious resources is being wasted, eradicated, each day. The rain forest scrubs the air we breathe, absorbs so much carbon dioxide through photosynthesis. And the burning puts much more carbon dioxide back into the air. Incredible ignorance. Incredible consequences.*

Jorge walked back into the waiting room very slowly, trying desperately to think of what he would tell Maria. He knew he must keep her from becoming too upset. She was going to have another child in three months, and she always got upset easier when she was with child. He decided it would do her no good to know that Gabriella might die.

Maria was asleep in the chair. Jorge bent close to her, gently placed his hand on her shoulder, whispered her name. She didn't stir. He shook her. "Gabriella?" She jumped to her feet from the chair, her face frozen with fear. Grabbing Jorge's arms, she squeezed them in an unconscious, vise-like grip.

"She is very ill, but she is breathing easier this morning. The doctor will not be able to tell us anything more until later. He was very nice. He said we should go and get some sleep and then come back."

"Is she going to die? Is Gabriella going to die?"

"She is very ill. But she is getting better because she is breathing easier this morning. Come with me. We must go and give the nurse information. We must also get the other children and bring them to the hospital so they can have medicine to keep them from getting sick like Gabriella."

The nurse asked them their names, ages, where they live, if Gabriella had ever been ill before, about their other children. Jorge was glad she was filling out the papers for them.

"When is your next child going to be born?"

"In three or four months," Jorge replied.

"Do you practice any type of birth control?"

The question stunned Jorge…left him with no idea how to answer. He thought he knew something about birth control, but he was sure the church was against it and Maria had such a strong belief. Turning to Maria he saw that her head was bowed. She could never talk about this.

"We are religious." Her head remained down as she answered the nurse.

"It is very dangerous for you to have any more babies after the one you are now carrying. There are many diseases such as the one that your daughter has that can make them very ill or kill them. Or kill you while you are with child."

Jorge stiffened and looked toward Maria. She was still looking down at the floor.

"Very young children and the mother are in particular danger." The nurse continued. "Your church does not want you to have children who will suffer and die...your church does not want you to take a chance on dying yourself. There is a method of birth control that your church approves of. You only have to have no sexual relations on certain days. Can you read?" She looked first at Jorge and then Maria.

"Yes." Jorge replied.

She handed him a small paper pamphlet. "Please read this and when you come back I will be glad to explain anything you do not understand." She smiled and her voice became soft. "It is important and God's wish that you have a healthy family and not have any more babies after the next one. And please bring your other children in as soon as you can so we can give them medicine to keep them from getting ill like your daughter. This is very important. They are in great danger, and you need to bring them in tomorrow or the next day. We will give you the medicine now."

Jorge felt great relief when the conversation came to an end and the nurse had not asked him to read any of the pamphlet while she was there.

"I want to go to a church here," Maria said as they walked back into the waiting room. "I want to go now and pray for Gabriella and the rest of our children."

It was Sunday morning and they found a church close to the hospital. There were only a few people scattered about the pews as it was between masses. They both knelt to pray. Jorge closed his eyes tightly and prayed harder than he ever had before. *God, please make Gabriella well and do not let my other children or my wife or me get sick with this horrible disease.*

Jorge was not accustomed to praying and could not think of anything else to say, so he said the same prayer again and again...he thought four or five times...before opening his eyes and glancing at Maria. She was still kneeling with her eyes closed, her rosary beads clutched tightly in her hands. He did not want her to think he was less concerned than she was, so he stayed on his knees with his head bowed and repeated his prayer again and again. Then he began to think about Maria.

When they lived in the city she would go to church each Sunday and on some days during the week. Since they left there had been no church close to them so she built a small shrine in their house and prayed in front of it every night. Not having a church was one of the things she did not like about living on their farm. Jorge knew they will have to move soon because the beans, corn and manioc did not grow as well the last two years as they did the first. He would find more land to clear that had better soil and Maria would again argue to go back to the city, but that is something he would never do. The tin shack, so little food, so many people crowded together...he cringed when he remembered these things. There was no work for him and the garbage and waste came into the shack when it rained.

His knees ached from kneeling. He had lost track of time while thinking, and he raised his head, opened his eyes, and sat back on the seat. Maria was still praying.

Jacinto Evangelista stopped the truck in front of the house and walked to the door. A boy of about twelve met him with a frightened expression on his face. There were smaller children standing behind him and Jacinto tried to calm them all with a broad smile.

"Hello, I am Jacinto. Is your father home?"

"No."

"Do you know when he will be back? I want to talk to him about your farm."

"He and my mother went to Porto Velho. My sister is sick and they took her to the hospital there. I do not know when they will be back."

"I will come again when they have returned. Is there anything you or your brothers or sisters need while they are gone? I will be glad to help you with anything that I can."

"No. We are fine."

"You have done a good job with your farm. How long have you lived here?"

"About three years."

"Good-bye. Tell your father I will come again to talk to him and give him this card," Jacinto said as he reached his hand out with his business card. The boy hesitated, then slowly reached to take it, coming no closer than the four or five feet that separated him from the visitor.

Jacinto turned the new diesel truck around and headed back towards B.R. 364. *Three years. Just what I guessed. The crops are poor, like they always are in the third year after the forest has been cut and burned. The soil in the rain forests in this part of Rondonia is very shallow and poor in nutrients once the magic fertilizer of the ash from the tree burnings has been spent. But farmers who clear their plots by cutting and burning don't know this, and when their first year's crop is plentiful they are encouraged. By the third or fourth year they are ready to move on and clear another farm, not realizing the same thing will happen again. But one man's misfortune can be another's gain. I will offer to buy this farmer's land for what is nothing to me but will seem a pot of gold to him. I will then have another 100 acres or so for the cattle ranch that is already cleared. I will make a large profit next year for the rich owners, who live in San Paulo, and, I have heard, the United States. And then they will give me a large increase in my salary.*

The morning was still early when they left the church. Jorge was very tired, and they parked the truck close to the hospital building to keep it out of the sun while they slept. Maria curled up in the cab and Jorge stretched out on the mattress in the bed of the old vehicle. He fell asleep immediately.

The sun, having now climbed above the building, was burning what felt like a hole through the left side of Jorge's cheek when he came awake. It took him a moment to remember where he was, and why, and then he looked into the cab. Suddenly frozen with fear, his eyes began frantically searching the parking lot, but there was no sign of Maria. *Would she go to the hospital without me? Has she found out about Gabriella?* Again he looked into the cab. An icy current crawled through his skin and his stomach knotted. A large stain of dark red was on the middle of the seat.

Jorge jumped over the side of the truck and ran as fast as he could around the corner to the entrance to the hospital. Slowing to a fast walk when he entered, he stopped completely in the waiting room. The same blank faces greeted him, and there was no sign of Maria. Moving quickly, pushing the now familiar doors open, he headed for the nurses desk.

The nurse was talking to someone and did not look up. He waited with his hat wrapped tightly in his hands, panting from the run and shaking, sweat running down his round, flat, deeply lined face framed by coal black hair and a wispy mustache. After what seemed to Jorge like too long a wait, the nurse glanced his way. She looked startled when she first saw the small man in front of her, but asked in a calm voice what he was there for.

"Doctor, is Doctor...." Jorge could not remember the doctor's name. "My daughter, she is very ill and my wife, I cannot find her. Do you know..."

"Please wait here." The nurse cut him off and disappeared around the corner.

Jorge could not think clearly. He tried, but his mind was confused, there were too many different thoughts, and then he heard a piercing scream start from the end of the hall. It moved through him, filled all the space around him. He closed his eyes.

"Lord God, Please make Gabriella well and please let Maria..."

"Jorge." The doctor was standing in front of him, and Jorge desperately searched his eyes for an answer. They were soft.

"Your daughter is going to be all right."

Jorge stared, motionless.

"Your wife is also going to be all right."

"But what did my wife, where is she? What is...?"

"She came in about an hour ago, to go to the bathroom. And realized she was bleeding, but it is nothing serious. She is very scared though, Jorge. You must be calm so you can go and assure her everything is going to be all right. You can also see your daughter now. And Jorge, as soon as you have seen them you must go and bring your other children so that we can give them the medicine."

The humans' blueprints, their DNA, are 99.99% identical, but there is a vast difference in their mental capabilities. Legacy must play a role, surely lack of education, and influence from other humans with lens that are distorted. So many with excellent mental capabilities and knowledge take many actions that are harmful - for themselves, other humans and the planet. And many others, without the mental capability or knowledge, and often with the best of intentions, also take many damaging actions. The cumulative effect is devastating. I, Luggalor.

2000

CHARLESTON, SOUTH CAROLINA

Jennifer sat at the table and waited for Horace to be brought in. There were three other tables in the room, each with one chair on each side, and they were all occupied by inmates and their visitors. This was the sixth time - once every week - she had visited him, and it wasn't getting any easier. She reminded herself to act positive, to try to boost his spirits.

An officer led him in and the shudder ran through her, as always, when she saw the chains on his wrists and legs.

"Hi, Horace. How are you this week?"

"Hi, Mrs. Baker. I'm OK, I guess."

"I brought you some chocolate chip cookies. You know, the kind you like, those that Jeffrey's mother taught me to bake. It's about the only thing I can cook, and when I find someone who likes them and tells me so...I'm not about to let them off with the hook with just one batch. I don't get compliments on my cooking very often, so I'll keep bringing them if you'll keep telling me they're good, whether they are or not."

"Yeah, well I think they're real good. They're lots better than anything they have in here."

"Has your mom been here today?"

"Not yet. She'll probably be comin in a while."

"I talked to your attorney again. He thinks having Miss Rainey testify for you will really help. We're got a lot of people now who are going to help fight this thing and you're going to get off, I just know it. It will be obvious to the jury after they've heard all the testimony that you were acting in self defense, and that you're going to get your act together if you get another chance."

"I sure hope so Mrs. Baker. I just don't think I could stand it, bein here or at another prison for very long. It's real bad, you know, and people tell me all kinds of stuff. It's scary."

"Who tells you, Horace? What do they tell you?"

"Well, a couple of guys in the cell with me have done some pretty hard time at Jackson. One was in for armed robbery and one for manslaughter. Says he killed some dude with his bare hands that was messin with his lady. They say if I go up I'll be real popular. You know, for sex and stuff. They say I better get friendly with some of the big, mean dudes that ain't queer real quick, so they'll protect me or else they'll get me and I'll probably get AIDS. They say I'll have to pay em though."

"Pay who?"

"The guys to protect me. They also say there's lots of drugs up there. That people try to get you takin all sorts of stuff so they can make you do stuff, or pay em, you know. I don't want nothin to do with drugs again, Mrs. Baker. But if somebody's makin me take em, I don't know. It's scary, you know."

"I do know, Horace. I understand. I know it's scary. But you must listen to what I'm going to tell you. And you must believe me, OK?"

"OK."

"There's an excellent chance you're going to be acquitted on grounds of self-defense. We've got some good, respectable people who are going to stand up for you and the truth is it was self defense...that's what happened. You've got to believe in the system, believe it will work to help you. It was designed to protect innocent people like you. You've also got to keep your spirits up and forget about what you hear in this place. Don't you know they're trying to scare you? Don't you know it makes them feel tough, makes them feel important, to scare the hell out of you and act like they're bad dudes who have done hard time and know their way around Jackson.?"

"But they've been there."

"Maybe they have, maybe they haven't. It doesn't really make any difference, Horace. The only thing that makes a difference is that you get out of this and make something of your life...that you don't end up like them, where the only way you'll be able to get respect is to brag about doing serious time and knowing a lot about the inside of a prison. I'll tell you what being tough is...what cool is...what being bad is...what getting respect is. It's coming out of this thing ahead, not letting it get you down, not letting it beat you. Making something of your life. Making it count. That'll earn you more respect than all the gangs you can join, all the drug money you can spend, all the prisons you can own. And you can do it. You've got everything it takes, Horace. You're smart, you're a nice guy, you've got a mother and family who love you, and a lot of other people who care about you and want to see you make it. And you know what else? You're good looking."

Jennifer gave him a quick, wry smile, but her intensity quickly returned. "It's not going to be easy though...you're going to have to be tough as hell. Don't listen to people who don't want you to make it, and there are going to be a lot of them. You know why? Because they're jealous. They see you've got what it takes and that makes them real uncomfortable, makes them jealous as hell. Know why? Because if you make it then they have to either admit they can't or they'll have to try too. And they're not tough enough to do that, and they know it."

"Sometimes I think I'm gonna' be all right, that I can do like you say and get my life straightened out. Then other times...I think, man, I'm in real bad trouble and there ain't no way out."

"Look, you made a mistake by hanging with the wrong guys and letting them get you into some things you know you shouldn't have been involved with. And then you got real unlucky and ended up at the wrong place at the wrong time. But there are plenty of people who've been in some serious messes and ended up OK because they made up their minds to hang tough and they did. They did what it takes."

Horace stared at the table, didn't say a word. With his head still down he spoke softly. "Yeah, but I don't have too much confidence in myself sometimes. I mean, I don't do as well in school and talk as well and all, you know, as other guys that are probably goin to be successful."

"Horace, look at me...listen." Jennifer leaned her head across the table, until her eyes were very close to his. "I'm going to tell you the only reasons, and I mean the only reasons, it seems to you that school work is harder and that you don't speak as well as some other people. Your mother has had to work so hard that she hasn't had time to read you all the books and help you with your studies like some of the other kid's parents have. And maybe some of your teachers didn't encourage you like they should. And a lot of the kids you hang with are in the same boat and the way they talk influences the way you talk, and it's just different. There's nothing wrong with that. Now you damn well better remember what I'm about to tell you. It's true so help me God and it's the most important thing I'll ever say to you. You have the ability to learn anything, and speak any way, and act any way, and accomplish anything you want to. It's going to take some hard work since you didn't get as early a start as some other kids, but if you want to do it you can, and I'm ready to help you. I'm not going to tell you it'll be easy, but I am going to tell you can do it. You've just got to make up your mind and then be tough...be cool...get it done. Doing something meaningful with your life is the coolest thing you can ever do. You'll get more respect than you can imagine."

"I don't know, I mean, well, I'm black you know and that really does make a difference."

"No!..Horace!...you black? I'll be damned. I hadn't noticed." She stared into his eyes, waiting for him to flinch, or smile.

He looked totally confused at first, and then it came...a slight, uneasy grin.

"I'm not about to buy it, Horace. Not that. It's bullshit. Oh, sure, it's harder for you, no doubt about that. While a lot of us white folk have great grandparents who started traditions of being teachers, or doctors, or shop owners, or mechanics, yours were just getting out of chains and had to start from the bottom up with nothing but a lot of hate still around. And the generations since then haven't had it as good as they should, because a lot of the hate stayed. And you and I know it's still around. I and a lot of other white people are genuinely sorry about all that. But we can't do anything to change what happened, we can only help you overcome it. Sure, it's harder for you, but things have changed, there's opportunity now, and there's plenty of evidence that proves it. Don't use it as an excuse not to try, Horace. Too many blacks do that and sell themselves out."

Jennifer saw the guard approaching from behind Horace. She looked up, caught his eyes with hers before he could speak. "Just another moment, please, and we'll be through."

"That's all, mam. Just a moment. Time's really up right now."

"Thank you." She again leaned across the table, her face only inches from his, trying to make her eyes appear soft. "Give me your hands."

"But..."

"Come on, it doesn't bother me. Put them up here."

He laid them down gently, so the chains won't clang. She put her hands on top if his, with her fingertips spread across the metal. "I want you to promise me that you'll go back in there and keep your head up. I want you to feel good about yourself because you're going to make it out of this and you're going to be fine. If you start feeling down, you stay cool and get your confidence back, and you do it by remembering everything we talked about...that you're smart and a great guy, and tough, and you've got a good mama and family and lots of other people who love you and believe in you and are going to support you. All these things are going to help you make something of your life...they're going to help you get out of here, be a success, be respected and happy. I believe in you, Horace, and I'm going to hang in with you and do everything I can to help you. But you've got to let me help you. You've got to work with me and not let me down. I'm going to make it harder for you to fail than it is for you to succeed, because I'm going to ride your butt so hard that if you screw up you'll wish the hell you could spend the rest of your life in this place."

"All right, let's go, right now." The guard was back, his voice full of impatience.

"Thank you, officer, for those extra few minutes." Jennifer smiled warmly at the man.

"Have a good week. Call me anytime you want to." She stood up, turned and walked out the door so he didn't have to let her see him being led, shuffling in the chains, back to the cellblock.

2000

RONDONIA, BRAZIL

Jorge's emotions were mixed as he steered the truck down the dirt road. Excited about finding a new farm, he was confident that the land he would choose now would produce good crops for a long time. He would go farther into the forest this time and would check the soil more closely. He had enough money from the sale of his old farm to Mr. Evangelista to provide for his family until he could harvest a crop, and he also had enough to buy a new chain saw. But thinking of the chain saw reminded him of the long, hard days of clearing the forest and then burning it, of building another house, of starting over again. And then he thought of Maria and how she would keep complaining about not going back to the city. He stopped the truck, climbed out, and began to walk through the thick jungle.

I decided to assume my natural form. Of all the wondrous things I had seen on planet 1003, and there had been many, the rain forest is what I marvel at the most. I love the incredible variety of trees and vegetation and creatures, the assault of sights, smells and sounds. This would likely be my last chance to be in the forest, as I had been notified I would be leaving the planet soon.

My thoughts ran back to the first time I had been sent to planet 1003, many years ago according to the humans' calendar. The council had made a serious initial miscalculation....a very serious, very uncharacteristic miscalculation. I had been able to hear and see precisely what each of the humans could hear and see, but as I could not access their thoughts, there was no way to understand why so many of these creatures seemed to have so many diverse interpretations, of the same information, the same spoken and written words. The purpose of that trip had been to learn how and why things were evolving as they were on planet 1003. It had long been identified as one of the galaxy's most inhabitable bodies, and one that contained an endless variety of living things. But without being able to access their thoughts, and thus understand why so many of the humans acted in so many varied, often contradictory, bizarre and harmful ways, it made it impossible to understand the cause and effect of what was taking place on the planet. The Council was only able to verify the diversity of the physical properties and life, while becoming totally confused by the actions of the humans. They came away from the expedition learning almost nothing of what they had hoped to learn. And they grew very weary of my glowing descriptions of planet 1003's beauty and intrigue.

The Council went to work on the problem and determined that each human has a type of internal lens through which passes all of the sights, sounds and other information that is transmitted by their senses. But what passes out of the lens of each human, and the resulting thoughts instantaneously processed in the cognitive part of their brain, can be very different. These differences are due to filters that develop on the lens throughout each human's life, and in particular the early years of their life. Because of the filters, the data their brain processes often becomes distorted, and it is these distortions that can cause diverse and often flawed thoughts and actions by some humans, and undistorted thoughts and correct actions by others - relevant to similar circumstances and situations.

After a great deal of research - I heard it took the Council an unprecedented hour or more - they were able to duplicate the lens, and the filters, of every human on the planet. Of course they would have to send someone back to 1003, to actually use the lenses, learn what registers, and how it is interpreted by each human as each bit of information passes through the lens, is filtered, processed, each thought is formulated, and each action carried out.

And so I again came to be selected to travel to planet 1003. This was primarily due to my persuasive arguments that my previous experience firmly established me as the most qualified for this new expedition. This time I would not be limited to listening and observing, in my invisible state, to the words and actions of the humans, without a clue as to the origin of their often irrational nature. This time I would not be constantly puzzled by contra- dictions to accepted parameters of cause and effect. This time I would be able to access every thought that comes from data the senses gather and that then passes through the lens and filters. I would have a clear window into the thoughts and actions of each human.

It has seemed to work to perfection, and now the time is nearing for me to make the journey home. Can I go back to being Luggalor? My existence will be so different. Planet 1003 is so fascinating. The physical beauty and wonder of the incredibly intricate interrelationships between everything on the planet seem so ingeniously, perfectly designed, and to work so well...except, of course, for the humans. Why can't they be less destructive, less determined to move upstream against the laws of nature and balance that are well established with everything else on the planet...and in the universe. But I will miss the humans the most. I have developed a sincere sense of empathy for their confusion, struggles and suffering, and a longing for their ability to experience unmitigated, all-encompassing emotion. Why can't the beings of my planet feel and display a similar range and depth of feelings? Or any feelings? Soul is a word I have heard often as I have made my way, with the lenses, through the thousands of humans all over the planet selected for me to research. Under- standing this word had proven challenging...and enlightening in a number of ways. I know it is unlikely I will ever again return to planet 1003. Most of the data has been collected that would enable the Council to make their determinations, to solve the riddle of the chaos and discord. There are too many other galaxies, stars and their planets to explore...it wouldn't make sense to the council to return to this one again. I wondered if the next place I visited would have Bach fugues...worthless rumination.

Before returning to Jorge's lens, I wanted to let all the sights, sounds and smells of the forest flow through me once more. Lying back on a large green leaf, one piece of the soft, dank carpet on the jungles floor, I gazed at slivers of sunlight streaming through the tops of towering trees, and followed them until they disappeared into the dense vegetation below. The rain had just stopped, and steam billowed toward the great, green canopy. Enormous droplets of water, after pausing momentarily, slid off the edges of leaves and splashed to the ground. The fragrance and feel of clear, cool freshness, of rejuvenation, enveloped me.

I watched, and listened, to the hundreds of different species of insects living in each of the magnificent mahogany trees rising above me. Seeds floated down from branches into a small, gurgling stream, and the fish that would distribute them hid under giant lily pads measuring three feet across. A young tapir, resplendent with its white, horizontal stripes, ambled along just in front of me. Hanging from a limb above was a gray, three-toed sloth. Marveling at the rising chorus of faunal calls, I heard the solo soprano of a caterwauling jaguar take the lead. Columns of huge black army ants rose and fell as they marched from leaf to humus and across more leaves. A Reddish Brown Bongo drank pooled water with its sleek, horned beak, while on a branch above an emerald green Toucan perched, flaunting its flaming red and yellow bill. Staring at a delicate, lavender orchid, then an enormous, glorious, radiant blue Morpho butterfly, I was transfixed trying to take in every bit of the wondrous beauty and harmony surrounding me. The sudden, strident voice of a howler monkey shook me from my stupor. I must get back to the lens. I, Luggalor.

Jorge was stalking through the dense growth on the forest's floor, looking alternately up, then down, for any sign of a path he could follow, slashing at bushes and vines with his machete, pouring sweat in the stifling mid-day heat. *It will take even more hard work to cut and clear this farm than the last one because it will be larger and this forest is very thick. But I will have more months this time before the end of the dry season and the time comes to burn, and then plant. And this time I will have a chain saw.*

Jorge passed by a huge nest of Aedes mosquitoes, carriers of yellow fever, the sight passing through his lens without any recognition or resulting thought. There was the same absence of thought when he saw the toucan and the giant Morpho butterfly. He was thinking of the flames when the forest burns and the coffee crop he will grow.

2000

CHARLESTON, SOUTH CAROLINA

"Mrs. Secrist, you must understand that Randall is in no way incapable of doing well in his schoolwork. In fact it's quite the opposite. Your son is bright and has the ability to excel in all his subjects. His problems have to do with motivation and that can certainly be corrected, but the time to correct them is now."

"But Mrs. Baker, what can we do? We're a very loving family and we give him everything he needs, and then some."

"Do you get involved in his homework and his studying? Do you work with him every day, or know whether he has finished his assignments or not?" Jennifer's voice was firm, but she didn't want to appear to be lecturing Randall's mother.

"Well, we insist that he do his homework every night and that he study for his tests, but we're gone quite a bit in the evenings due to my husbands civic and company functions and, of course , there's the junior league, and the church meetings and suppers. You know, there just doesn't seem to be enough time any more. And then Randall seems to always get upset if we question him too much."

"I understand, Mrs. Secrist. Believe me, I do. But this time in Randall's life is very critical. It's a time when many young people can get themselves into trouble if they don't have the right amount of support, encouragement and applause. And I think applause is maybe the most important thing. You can show them what to do, sometimes even help them do it, but what really makes a difference is showing them you like what they have done, that you think they're terrific because they accomplished this or that, or that they at least tried. We're all the same, we all like to hear people tell us we're doing a good job. There are so many bad things a kid Randall's age can slip into these days without their parents ever knowing it, and I'm sure you know what those things are."

"Let me make a suggestion, Mrs. Secrist. I think if you or your husband would offer to help Randall every day with his homework and studying, really show an interest in what he's doing and not just whether or not he has completed it. Try to develop an interest in what he's learning, show you're interested, and I think you'll see a significant change for the better. Parents can learn a lot they missed the first time around through their involvement in their children's education. And show a sincere interest in his other activities, try to get involved with him in as many things as you can, and encourage him. He may have talents and interests you're not even aware of. I think you'll find he won't be as resentful or act as angry if you use this approach. It may take a little time because he's going to be leery at first, and it may be a bit uncomfortable for you and your husband, but if you stick with it and are sincere with your involvement in different aspects of his life - his grades will improve, I promise you. And as I said before, and this is so important, as he begins to improve tell him how proud you are of him. Tell him how great a student and a son he is. It'll make all the difference in the world and might also save you from some serious problems in the future."

"Thank you very much, Mrs. Baker. We'll do what you suggested and I'm sure his work will improve," Mrs. Secrist said, then turned and walked quickly from the classroom.

Last of the parent conferences. Glad that's over with. I'll bet Mrs. Secrist won't get involved for long, if at all. But maybe I'm being too hard on her, too judgmental. God, I hate that in other people. I don't really know her, just two meetings. Maybe she'll prove me wrong. Jennifer usually looked forward to the conferences and knew she would normally have taken more time with Mrs. Secrist, would have talked to her more about the need for parents to make sacrifices, do whatever it takes to enable them to play a more active role in different facets of their children's lives. But on this day she was on edge, impatient, out of sorts. It was because of what would happen the next day…she knew that.

Jan appeared in the doorway. "Have you talked to Larry Davis again?"

"Not since Monday," Jennifer said, "but I already told you about that. Maybe we should take his advice and not worry. He sounded confident we'll have all the time we need to go over our testimony at the courthouse before the trial starts. I thought about calling him again last night but I decided against it. Jeffrey said he thinks the guy knows what he's doing, that he probably already knows all he needs to and would just tell us to be calm, listen, think before we respond, and speak clearly. I told Jeffrey I was glad all the time he spent in front of the TV watching L.A. Law was finally paying off with such an incredibly unique insight into efficient courtroom behavior. He didn't smile."

"Well, I don't know," Jan said, "it's just the image I have of public defenders. And it's probably not fair."

"It may not be, but I think about it too. I will say though, that when we met he impressed me as someone who is very dedicated to what he is doing and that he understands the importance of it all. He also sounded as if he had really listened to Horace and had a feel for what he's all about. I still wish we could have found some way to hire a good private attorney though."

"I guess we should remember what the alternatives were," Jan says, "Davis has got to be better than that shmuck Mrs. Wilson found."

"Yeah, and he might have been the cream of the crop of guys who will try a case like this for $5000.00 max, guaranteed, with an installment plan. Can you imagine?" Jennifer laughed.

"I can imagine he should have just gone ahead and also said $5000.00 minimum, guaranteed," Jan said.

"I'd better go. On the excellent chance that I really did piss Jeffrey off this morning, I'll try to make amends by preparing a true gourmet dining experience complete with candlelight and Mozart. Ragu de le vase extraordinaire. I get sooo many compliments."

Jennifer stepped into Mr. Holder's office on her way out. "See you in court tomorrow." She wanted to remind him one more time, let him know once again how much they needed him to be there, how much they were counting on him.

"I'll be there. Let's hope everything works out."

Jennifer was out of the shower and downstairs with the paper and a cup of coffee at 6 a.m., thirty minutes before the alarm would have awakened her. She had slept little and finally decided to stop fighting it, although she realized the lack of rest was going to compound the irritability and nervousness she felt.

"Morning, hon," Jeffrey said as he walked into the kitchen at 6:45.

"What's this about Huntington latex paint being found with mercury in it?" Jennifer's voice was sharp. "There's a big article in the paper. Says it's a direct violation of HUD standards that have been in effect for years."

"Can't you at least say good morning before you begin the inquisition. It's no big deal, just some left over inventory that went out by mistake. The content's real low anyway."

"Did you know about this?"

"Yeah, but..."

"Jeffrey, you knew about this. They found this stuff in twenty different stores. Mercury affects kid's kidneys, IQ's and reactions. When did you know about it?"

"Look, it's still legal in exterior paint so that tells you something about the danger right there. Somehow the old interior stuff got into the pipeline and into the stores before we realized it. The content is low. It's not that much of a danger."

"That's crap, and you know it. It's probably more dangerous than we've been told. Thousands of kids will end up licking the walls and eating the chips...and painters will pour the leftovers into the dirt and it will get into the ground water and kids eat dirt you know. If you knew they were selling paint with mercury in it, why didn't you go and tell somebody?"

"We didn't realize it until it was already out and being used. We knew what the press would do and thought some people might panic if we recalled it; and, like I said, the content is real low. I didn't make the decision and I really don't think it would have been in my best interest to go to Frank with my Ralph Nader impression. The press is making a much bigger deal out of it than it really is."

"Jesus, Jeffrey. Not in your best interest?" You know you're endangering people and breaking the law and all you're concerned about is what Frank will think. I'm sure you can find a job with a company that's a little more concerned about children's health. You're the comptroller, how much would you have lost if you had recalled it? That's it, isn't it, or maybe the money and the bad P.R."

"That's enough, please. I think you're out of line with this."

"You guys just don't learn, do you? It hasn't been but a couple of months since you tried to build a new plant on protected wetlands...Christ."

"Jennifer, you know the government reclassified that land as available for restricted development."

"Sure, Jeffrey, but the conservatives have decided that everything that's not under five feet of water at low tide is arid and more deserving of K-MARTs and condos than the thousands of species that use it for breeding grounds and a habitat."

Jennifer got up and stormed upstairs to the bathroom to put her makeup on and finish getting ready. She stared in the mirror. *All right, calm down. This isn't the way to start this day. I've got to be poised and articulate and sound very sincere. Breathe deep...relax.*

Jennifer walked up the steps to the courthouse at 8:30, thirty minutes before Horace's attorney, Larry Davis, told her to be there. After finding the designated courtroom, she leaned her back against the wall and watched, as the hall gradually came to life. Some waited as she did, others scurried about and appeared to be moving with a definite purpose, still others stood and talked amicably, even jovially, with animated greetings and gestures. It seemed a number of these people knew each other, and the business at hand wasn't unduly concerning them. No one looked as uptight as she felt.

Horace's mother arrived at 8:50. "Hello, Mrs. Wilson." Jennifer smiled warmly and extended her hand.

"Hello, Mrs. Baker. I'm real nervous Mrs. Baker, and I talked to Horace last night and he said he hadn't slept hardly at all the last few nights. He's real nervous too."

"I know he is, but we've got to believe everything's going to work out and he's going to beat this thing." Jennifer looked straight into the woman's eyes. "I really believe it's going to be all right, Mrs. Wilson, I really do."

Jan walked up and greeted them both.

"Well, I'm going to go on in and get a seat," Mrs. Wilson said, "I don't go to church regular, you know, but I've been prayin a lot these last few days. It'll just kill him, and me too, if he has to stay in jail much longer." She turned and walked through the heavy, ornate, wooden door.

"God," Jan said, "This might be a bitch. I'm not so sure I'm emotionally equipped for this sort of thing."

86

"Yeah, me either," Jennifer answered.

"Have you seen his attorney?" Jan asked.

"No, I did finally call him last night but he didn't say anything he hadn't said before. He told me he'd meet us here a little before nine."

"How about Horace?" Jan said in a quiet voice.

"No, they wouldn't let me talk to him. Rules and regulations, you know. The day his whole life is going to turn on, he's scared to death, and he can't even have a phone call."

Larry Davis, Horace's court-appointed attorney, appeared in the hall and walked toward the two women. "Is Mrs. Wilson here yet?" His voice had urgency in it.

"Yes, she's inside." Jennifer replied.

"We need to get her and talk, I've got a deal, but I've got to get back with Judge Elder soon."

"A deal?" Jennifer's voice was loud and full of alarm. "What do you mean a deal? What kind of deal?"

"Listen to me Mrs. Baker, please." Davis's tone was calm, the words measured. "The judge has agreed to reduce the charge to manslaughter. He'll be sentenced to ten years and he'll be eligible for parole in three."

"Goddamn it, you just plea bargained his life, didn't you? And you didn't even ask anybody about it? Not his mother, not me, did you even ask him?" Jennifer felt a red heat exploding within her, knew she was losing control.

"Of course I asked him. He has to plead guilty. I met with him this morning. He understands and agrees it's his best chance, the safest way to go."

"He agreed because you talked him into agreeing. Isn't that right? He's scared to death, you know that, and he's intimidated with someone like you throwing legal jargon at him. Christ...I can't believe this. He's innocent, and that would have come out in that courtroom. He shot that boy in self defense and there's no reason he should spend another night in jail. You're ruining his life, don't you know that? You know what will happen to him if he ends up in prison."

"Mrs. Baker, please calm down. Please calm down and listen to me." Again the attorney's voice was calm, but this time it carried more force.

Jennifer looked at Jan and saw a confused, helpless expression on her face. Jan put her hand around Jennifer's arm and looked at Davis. "Can we get out of this hall to talk?"

Davis led them around the corner and into an empty courtroom. He motioned them onto one of the back benches, then sat on the bench in front of theirs and turned back to face them.

By outward appearance Jennifer was calmer, but she still seethed. She stared at the attorney, waited for him to speak.

"You believe Horace is innocent and I do too, believe me," Davis started, "but making the jury believe that is a completely different matter. He was on a street corner to sell crack. He was a member of a gang. He was armed. He's admitted all that. He shot and killed somebody and the only eye witness says it wasn't self defense. The jury doesn't know what a great guy he is, and believe me the district attorney will do everything he can to keep them from finding out."

"But the..."

"Please, Mrs. Baker, let me finish. There's a lot of anti-drug sentiment in this town and, I'm sure you've noticed, some racism. People are frightened. Juries do funny things. Even when a case is airtight, they can surprise the hell out of you, and this case is far from airtight. All we've got is his testimony and the testimony of his teachers and mother that he couldn't possibly have done it. And I'd be nervous about putting him on the stand. If he's intimidated by me you can imagine what the cross examination could be like. He could really do himself in."

"The boy who's going to testify against him, you said he's got a record a mile long?" Jennifer asked.

"True, but that will likely never come out in court. He's under indictment too, for Andy's death."

"He's getting a deal to testify, of course, to lie about what happened, isn't he?" Jennifer asked.

"I'm not his attorney. I don't know."

"Well, I damn well know." Her voice rose again.

"Sentencing guidelines have been strengthened in the last few years for serious crimes like this, and judges don't have the leeway to go light if there's some doubt or it's a first offense." Davis looked over at Jan and then back at Jennifer. He paused. "If Horace is convicted, and I think there is a reasonable chance he would be, he could end up being sentenced to a minimum of twenty years, and have to serve ten or more. You've got to look at the odds. This is a good deal considering the circumstances."

"Why didn't you tell us you were trying to make a deal? You're deciding his future, his whole life, because that's what it amounts to, and you didn't even consult us." Jennifer's voice had risen in a steep crescendo, and she was screaming. "Goddamn it, this is unbelievable."

"I did mention it to you, the first time we met, but you made it clear you didn't want to hear anymore. And I didn't know until this morning that I could pull it off. I get twenty five new cases a week that I try to do the best I can with, Mrs. Baker." Davis's tone suddenly took on an edge of irritability. "And I think I've done a good job here. I don't have the luxury of calling everyone associated with each of my defendants and giving them up-to-the-minute briefings."

"Is the deal done, Mr. Davis?" Jennifer's words came quickly.

"I need to talk to Mrs. Wilson and then get back with the judge."

"I would like to talk to the judge. I want to talk to him before you talk to Mrs. Wilson."

"That would be highly irregular, Mrs. Baker. He's about to go into court and..."

"Look," Jennifer said, interrupting him, "I've been as close to this as anybody. I've spent a lot of time with Horace. I'm a concerned citizen, Mr. Davis. Isn't that what we're supposed to need more of? I think you can arrange it if you try." She brought the full force of her stare onto him, and hoped he realized what she wouldn't accept.

Davis paused a moment before speaking, as if to take the full measure of her. "The two of you wait outside. I'll see what I can do."

Jan broke the silence when they were back in the hall. "Maybe he's right."

Jennifer stared at the floor. "Goddamn, Goddamn it."

After only a few minutes Larry Davis came around the corner and motioned to them. They walked into the judge's chambers and Jennifer felt her face flush as the judge peered at her over his reading glasses. She knew she was good looking and glad of it, but it infuriated her when the first thing a man does is look her up and down. The judge didn't even try to hide it as most men so unsuccessfully do.

"Your honor, this is Jennifer Baker and Jan Bond. They're Horace Wilson's teachers," Davis said, introducing them.

Jennifer walked forward to accept the hand of Judge Elder. *Stay calm, keep cool, convince this son-of-a-bitch.*

"Your Honor, Horace Wilson will be destroyed if he goes to prison. His cellmates are already telling him how often he's going to be raped and forced to buy drugs. He's a nice, shy kid who's easily influenced and got mixed up with the wrong people, ended up at the wrong place at the wrong time, and then had to act in self-defense. He never intended to hurt anyone. He's never been in trouble before. He's got a mother and family who care deeply about him and other people like Jan and I who are willing to work with him and help him. He's bright and can make something of himself if he's just given a chance."

Jennifer paused for a moment, trying to gage the judge's reaction. His expression didn't change...there were no clues.

She continued. "I used to teach in an inner-city school in Chicago. Eighty percent of the kids were from projects. I saw it all too often...once they spent enough time around the wrong people or in some kind of lockup, the chances of saving them dropped dramatically. If there's anything you can do to help Horace...anything, your Honor...you'll be saving any chance he has at a decent future." Moisture formed in her eyes as she stopped speaking and stared at Judge Elder.

"You're very eloquent, Mrs. Baker, and obviously sincere and dedicated to your pupils. I admire that. But you must understand that I have already done something for Horace Wilson. It's not my job to decide his guilt. A jury does that. What I can do is reduce the charges in certain cases where I feel the circumstances warrant it and that is what I have done here. The only way he can avoid prison is to be found not guilty...and to be honest, his chances of that aren't good. If he is found guilty, my hands will be more severely tied than they are now. Second degree murder carries a stiff sentence."

"This system is breaking down all around us, Mrs. Baker. There are too many crimes committed, too many people waiting for trial, and too many that are convicted and must be put in overcrowded prisons. There are not enough attorneys like Mr. Davis who will do this work, and the time or money to explore every case the way they did on Perry Mason just isn't there. The press howls about the fact that the courts are unfair to the poor, but no one is willing to pay to do anything about it. Horace Wilson is getting a fair shake under the circumstances and the system. Now I must go to court."

Jennifer and Jan walked out of the courthouse into the glare of a bright November sun. They did not speak until Jan asked Jennifer if she was all right.

"Yeah, I'm O.K. I'll see you back at school." Jennifer turned and walked across the street to the parking lot. She got in her car, closed the door, rested her head on the steering wheel, and sobbed.

Some of the humans care so deeply about other humans...others don't appear to care at all...and so many of the less fortunate are so gravely harmed by the latter that they can't be helped by the former . I, Luggalor.

2000

NORTHERN PACIFIC

Coming awake suddenly...gasping for air...Li lurched up in the berth and felt an explosion of pain as his head cracked into the pipe directly overhead. Probably the tenth time it had happened during the past two weeks. A slight sense of claustrophobia was partly to blame, but more so the insanely small berths and lack of head room. It seemed there was nothing around his head to breathe when he awakened in the stale cabin at night. He looked at the time - 4:15 a.m. There was another hour until his watch began and he knew he would not be able to fall back asleep. Deciding not to try, he kept his eyes open, listening to the deep throb and drone of the diesels, feeling their vibrations course through his body like a incessant, pulsating charge. The constant noise, vibrations, and smell of fuel were the worst part of the first three days, when he felt more miserable than he ever had at sea. The pitching and rolling he could handle...but down below, it was unbearable. He was adjusting, but he would always hate those engines. Li wondered what today would bring in the huge nets. They were nearing the zone south of the Aleutians where the squid would be...and dolphins, whales, salmon and birds.

Li recalled his first time on the ocean in a ship. It was many years ago, but only two days after he had escaped the slaughter at Tiananmen Square in his native China through Hong Kong. He sailed aboard a freighter to Tokyo, then on another to the U.S. Those vessels were plush compared to the old fishing vessel he was on now. Recalling those long days on the passages, he thought of the hours he spent meticulously planning his return to China and his strategy for continuing to work to change the system and the leadership. After reaching the U.S. and learning all that was going wrong in his homeland...he was devastated. Every bit of progress that had been made was evaporating. Many people, among them his friends and the country's brightest young minds, were being imprisoned and executed. He realized how lucky he was to escape. His sister, who had been by his side at Tiananmen, had not been as lucky. She was separated from him in the chaos of that dreadful night...and, he heard, was in prison.

After months of depression he also realized it was futile to realistically expect any reversal of the crackdown and renewed political oppression in the foreseeable future. At least until the current leadership died off, or the international community applied enormous pressure. And they wouldn't. Even with the beacon of revolutions in Eastern Europe, the leadership had too firm a grip, too much power, and were too determined to stop at nothing to continue their system of privilege. Their greed and commitment to self preservation was too strong. Freedom would eventually come, he was sure of it, but he could envision nothing more that he could do at the time. It was so unreal to him. His country had made more positive strides than any other major socialist nation in the fifteen years leading up to the massacre. Measures utilizing principles of a market system and allowing ownership and profits for productivity had vastly improved the economy and promised much more progress in the years ahead. An incredibly successful, national family planning program had cut the population growth of the world's most populous nation by one half, and while the number of newborns declined significantly, the infant mortality rate also fell due to improvements in education and medical care. China was poised to show the world that an enlightened hybrid of socialism and capitalism could work.

When the students started the demonstrations they were not advocating the overthrow of the socialist system, or even the present government. They were merely calling for less corruption and more progressive political measures to go along with the new economic freedom. They were not armed. The demonstrations and the occupation of the square had none of the violence that would normally be associated with a serious threat to a government as entrenched as the one in Beijing. But nonetheless, all the progress and promise and hopes were wiped out by as ruthless and bloody a crackdown as one could imagine under any provocation. A generation of the country's best minds and talents were lost to flight, imprisonment, or death. And all because of the greed of a group of leaders and bureaucrats, who were consumed with fear at losing even a portion of their lavish privileges and license for corruption. It amazed Li that so many people, under so many communist regimes, and for so long, had lived with the hardships of these systems, brainwashed into thinking it was for their own good and the good of the nation.

Eventually he came to the conclusion that he must become involved in something else meaningful, another honorable cause, if he was to lose his despondency, and so he set out to become an environmental journalist. He traveled, researched and wrote in relative obscurity for years, rarely getting his angry articles published in well-known or widely read publications. That changed with recognition for an article he wrote chronicling the clubbing deaths of harp seal pups in the Arctic, and a huge commercial hunt using the same method on gray seal pups in Africa - a practice widely thought to have ended years before. Writing with less venom than in his previous narratives, he emphasized reasons and solutions. The recognition also led to a position as a regular contributor to the magazine 'The Environmentalist'. Over the recent years, as environmental abuses and problems received more and more attention, he became increasingly dedicated to what he was doing. China was once again making real progress on a number of fronts...but still had serious problems related to political and human rights and corruption. He would go back someday and help with the necessary changes to the system that he knew had only been delayed, but for now he knew nothing was as important to as many people as the environment and protecting it.

This assignment would fill the month he had free before his

next assignment He had signed on as a deckhand aboard an unmarked vessel out of Taiwan suspected of salmon poaching and indiscriminate drift net fishing for squid in protected waters south of the Aleutians. Drift net methods had received a lot of criticism in the early part of the eighties, and some countries had outlawed them or boycotted the products they produced. But, as with anything that involves large profits, it was hard to control completely and for long. Rumors were numerous that the abuses had become serious again.

The alarm on his wristwatch began its high-pitched beep, and he rolled off his berth. Pulling on the heavy, yellow oilskins, Li walked toward the galley for a cup of tea before going on deck.

After inhaling one cup and most of another, he grabbed the rails, pulled himself up the metal, grated stairway, and entered the cold, wet world on deck. The morning's first, faint light was enough to show that the gray, rainy skies of the past two days were still above them. The rain was light at the moment, practically a mist, but the wind was blowing much harder than it had on his previous watch. A damned unpleasant environment, and the thought of working in these conditions for the next six hours was not helping his tired, irritable mood. He heard an unusual number of voices through the wind as he walked forward, and as he reached the deck he realized why. Squid ink was everywhere, and a mass of quivering fish filled the deck. There were hundreds of squid but also salmon, tuna, and a large shape in the corner that he knew instinctively was a Right Whale. Li glanced quickly around to be sure no one had seen him, and they had not...they were far too busy. Moving quickly aft and back down the stairway, he headed for his bunk. Again he looked to see if anyone was watching. From a bag under the thin mattress he removed the tiny video camera, then fed the four-foot long flexible shutter trigger that he had fashioned through the arm of his jacket. Slipping the camera into a bracket sewn into the inside of the large pocket on the side of his coat, he attached it to the trigger, then reached up his left sleeve with his right hand and pulled the cable until the end was at his cuff. Straightening his arm, he assumed a relaxed, nonchalant stance and depressed the knob on the end of the trigger cable with only a very slight movement of the three fingers of his left hand. He glanced at the camera in his pocket...and saw the green light was on. A smile crossed Li's face as he closed the pocket of his jacket, turned, and again headed for the deck.

Any pleasure or excitement he felt about his ingenuity and the promise of what the camera would document was quickly erased by the sight that slammed into his eyes as he stepped back into the howling maelstrom. The lights were still on, and through the gloom they cast a garish, milky yellow illumination on a sickening scene. Two dolphins were caught in the net and one of the crew was cutting off the beak of one to remove it. Li pushed open the slit in his pocket and activated the trigger. Stiffening, he watched the sleek, light gray body writhe, the spurt of bright scarlet, and heard its scream rise in pitch until it was almost imperceptible. The beak fell away and the dolphin, blood covering its head, was tossed to the deck. Scanning the writhing mass, Li was horrified. There were eight or ten other dolphins on the deck and two babies. The Right Whale was young, and there was an even smaller calf next to it. There were three seals, two sea turtles, and a number of forked-tail sea petrels. And literally hundreds of sockeye and Coho salmon. He panned the deck, forcing himself to take more time than he wanted to. When he was convinced he had recorded the whole wretched scene, he closed the slit, released the trigger, jumped down onto the deck and ran for the baby dolphins. Throwing the first one overboard, he knew that its chances of survival without its mother were nonexistent, so he grabbed the arm of a crewman and motioned for him to help lift the mother dolphin over the side.

The man turned and yelled to be heard over the wrenching screech of the huge power blocks as they pulled the net in. "There is no time now. There is too much in the nets. We will do it later."

Desperately looking around for other help, Li realized it was futile. The mammals would die soon...they had been out of the water for some time. He knew he must work or he would cause suspicion. Moving to his station, he began to pull fish from the thin, monofilament mesh of the gigantic, 30 mile long net as it was winched aboard. The full meaning of the term 'walls of death' was clear to him now. *Any creature that swims into these invisible nets or is ensnared by them is doomed. It is so indiscriminate, so wasteful. All that is sold are the squid and the illegal salmon... everything else is an innocent casualty of this ghastly, prolific harvester of sea life. But the owners of this catch are going to pay a heavy price.* Li tried to numb his mind for the hours of brutal, illegal work ahead.

This photographer has a sense of the harmony among all life in the universe necessary to sustain life...life that evolves to fit into the grand scheme.

I had received an urgent message from the Council that I must return by the end of this day on Planet 1003. There was an issue that could not be ignored on Planet 3683, and after a short stop I would be on my way there. I had not found the Wise One, and the only consolation was that I would likely need to return in order to complete that crucially important aspect of my missions to Planet 1003. I stayed in my human form so that I could feel the intense sorrow that came over me as I thought about leaving. Sorrow wasn't a pleasant human emotion, but I reveled in the intense feelings that coursed through me with any of their emotions. Even those that were unpleasant. Along with the Bach Fugues, I would miss the emotions as much as any of the fascinating mysteries of the humans' behavior, and the magnificent beauty of their planet. I, Luggalor.

2012

IRAN

Saleh was terrified, but knew he must show no fear as he sat in the front room of the small, concrete house. Safia, his eighteen year old sister, cried hysterically and pleaded with their father.

"Come with me now." Dahab, his father, spoke to her in a stern voice.

"Please, not that, not that. I beg you. Strangle me, I beg you."

"Have you no shame at all. You knew it would be done. Come, it is time."

His father, mother and older sister led the sobbing Safia to a back room. Saleh wanted to run outside but knew he would be seen. Pressing his hands over his ears, he squeezed tightly. He closed his eyes. His palms glistened with sweat, and he could feel his heart beating wildly inside his chest. Then he realized he could not be seen like this, cowering like a dog, so he opened his eyes and put his hands down...and waited...paralyzed with fear, not moving, not thinking...just waiting. Finally he heard the door open and watched his father walk out of the room and towards him....blood pouring from the severed head of Safia as he carried it in his hands. And then he saw her eyes...ghastly, wide open.

Dahab went outside and Saleh could hear him bellow out to the villagers, "I have killed her. I have washed the stain from my family."

The villagers came into their house for the next few hours and went to the back room to view Safia's body. The women filed in slowly, with heads bowed. The men shook Dahab's hand and congratulated him, speaking in soft voices. His father wore a look of great relief.

Saleh was awake each moment of the night. His mind raced, his thoughts jumped, but continued to return to the terrifying image of the severed head of his sister, and with the image an electric current of a shudder ran through him again and again. He tried not to think about never seeing his sister alive again, but he understood why.

The teachings started in early childhood. His family was part of a Bedouin tribe that lived by a strict code of honor and blood revenge for anyone bringing shame on the family or tribe. They were also fundamentalist Sunni Muslims, and believed in obeying the word of the Imams, and the laws of Sharia, to the letter, and at all times. The more militant Imams encouraged swift revenge for any loss of honor on the family, tribe, or nation…and the bloodier the revenge the more cleansed were the disgraced. Thus he had known what would happen from the minute Safia and their mother returned from the doctor with the news that she was with child. There was no greater stain that can be brought on a family than to have an unwed daughter with child. His father did the only thing he could to restore their honor and the honor of the tribe.

The next day Saleh went with his family to bury Safia. Her corpse was not washed or shrouded as is normally required by Islamic law, and no one said prayers over her body during the burial. Everything she owned and all the pictures of her had been burned. There was nothing left to remind the village, or her family, of Safia.

As the body was dumped into the unmarked grave, Saleh felt tears fill his eyes. But he knew he must be strong and act like a man. In one week he would be sixteen and go to Damascus to join Hezbollah. After training he would go to fight the Zionists in the Jihad and avenge the shame and suffering they have brought to the Arab people and all Muslims. His father was proud of him and would be very upset if he saw him crying. Saleh thought how different their deaths would be…his and his sister's…if he was fortunate enough to die a martyr for such a noble and holy cause.

How incredibly distorted the reasoning ability of humans can become through evil influences. Their perspectives can be so fragile, so easily corrupted, particularly when they are young...or if they are less than well educated. I, Luggalor.

2012

TEL AVIV, ISRAEL

General Mark Engen anticipated the worst as he waited with the two other generals, the chief of staff, and the defense minister. They were awaiting the arrival of the chief of the Mossad. The head of the elite intelligence agency didn't usually give briefings directly to field officers. The information was normally given to those up the line and then disbursed, but this was an exception, and he knew that the exception was as good a testament as any to the gravity of the situation. He had been told that a Katsa, or case officer, had just sent the latest dispatch on planned troop strengths and movements, and the deployment of artillery and missiles. Time was too critical for it to filter through the usual chain, and he presumed they wanted some immediate feedback from those in the room.

Engen tried to recall when he first knew it would come to this. *The fundamentalist uprisings and political changes among the Arab nations that intensified after the millennium and the attacks of 9/11 shifted the attention away from Israel's security. Afghanistan eventually fell again to the fundamentalist Taliban because the U.S. didn't finish them off when they could have in the initial post 9/11 campaign, and this emboldened fundamentalists in other countries in the region. The Saudi's began to look weak. The world was so anxious to stabilize the area and the oil fields that the legitimate concerns of Israel were subverted for the expediency of finding a quick fix to the situation. The lines of a Palestinian state were drawn, and we could no longer closely control the territory adjacent to Israel. Compared with the radical Islamic threat, Palestinian rule probably looked good to the West. America's failed war replaced the menace of a secular Saddam with an eventual Islamic leadership in Iraq that Iran and Syria could dominate. Pakistan's victorious fundamentalist regime, laced with the Taliban and Qaida sympathizers, supplied the missing link for the nuclear component, and the final piece of the puzzle fell into place with the coup in Saudi Arabia and enemy confiscation of the huge cachet of high-tech weaponry Washington had recently shipped. The suddenness of the situation caught everyone off guard, except the Mossad. The Americans, with a hotly debated, mostly reactionary policy, and pressure from the Arab world to pull back, would not listen. From that point on it was just a matter of time until Israel's worst nightmare came true - a united Arab front moving against us with enormous troop strength, a direct route in, substantial and sophisticated air, artillery and missile capability, chemical and biological weapons, and verified nuclear warheads.*

He considered the grim choices. *A preemptive strike will be much more difficult than it had been in 67', or on the reactor at Osirak. Losses are guaranteed to be much heavier, if, indeed, it is at all successful. If the birds do get through and threaten to take out a lot of their capability it will tempt them to immediately trigger the chemicals, bios or even the nukes rather than lose them on the ground. We can wait and hope the Americans get off their asses, their President has the balls to act, and they get some more people over here in time to do some good. More F22's, 16's, and Stealths would also help, particularly if a lot are lost at the beginning, but what we really need are tanks and troops to keep the bastards from overrunning the place if we can't stop them early. And then there is the other move, a nuclear first strike.* He still shuddered when he could bring himself to actually contemplate it.

Simon Meloman, chief of the Mossad, entered the room and Minister of Defense Isaiah Perlman and Lieutenant General Yosi Perin rose to greet him. Everyone was acknowledged, Meloman opened his attaché case, removed some papers, and began to speak.

"Gentlemen, the news is not promising. There are plans to

move two more divisions from Iran just to the west of Manhattat Unayzah, another from Syria and one from Iraq to just north of Tyre. That will put 200,000 men and 1200 tanks and all the usual support to our southwest, 250,000 and 1,500 to the west, and 100,000 and eight hundred to our north. There will be additional 122 mm's and 152's moved in and the usual compliment of SA 13's 14's, SCUDS and SS 21's and 23's. There is no indication that this is the end, either. There should be more SCUD batteries moving into southwestern Syria but the information on where and when is sketchy. And there is still a lot of troop movement within Iran and Iraq, but nothing detailed on any more deployments."

General Perin, Chief of Staff, spoke first. "That's going to stretch us unless we can kill a lot of their equipment up front. If we mobilize everybody we can just stay with them now. We have superiority in the tanks, but the numbers are getting closer and we know they've got another 3,000 or more they can bring in. Mark, what do you think?"

"I agree we still have a good chance to stop them if the planes and artillery can get a good jump, but if they bring up much more armor and troops we could have real problems. In any case it's going to be messy."

"Benjamin, how about you?" Perin turned to the head of the air force.

"We can still mortally wound them with a first strike, but we need to move now, before they have any more SAMS and guns in place. And I would concur with Mark. It's going to be a mess."

"Martin?"

"I don't see how we can just sit and wait for them to keep deploying and overpower us," Martin Sharar, chief of naval operations, answered without any hesitation.

"Well, gentlemen, the reason we are waiting, of course, is the U.S. They still think they can pressure the U.N. to do something other than continue to issue warnings. We keep telling them there isn't any reason to think the U.N. is going to act before the fact and until it's too late. They keep telling us to wait one more day. For all the U.N.'s recent history of movement in the right direction, there are new problems caused by their more active involvement that could be catastrophic in our case. The U.S. hesitates to act unilaterally any more without giving them a good long chance to do something. And since Russia's determined to join the U.S. in defusing every major crisis, they also have to wait the hell to let them play their part and get in on the glory. The way things are now may be better for their image and politics back home, but a couple of years ago they could have acted and given us what we needed without having to wait and risk seeing this whole region go up. Simon, do you have any more on where the nukes are, and the chemicals and bios?"

"Same information as yesterday. There are chemicals and bios scattered throughout, but more around Tyre. The nukes we just don't know. We hope to have something soon. God, would that help."

"Thank you, Simon." Perin and Perlman stood and shook Meloman's hand, and the Mossad chief walked quickly from the room.

Benjamin Gaifen spoke up. "Yosi, if we can locate theirs, it seems like we've got to go ahead and send ours. I mean, it looks like we might be left to go this thing alone. If that's the case, the hell with everyone else. We have to do what we know will give us the best chance to survive, as we've always done. We know they have nukes and we know of three or four scenarios where they will probably use them. In fact, it seems there isn't much of a chance they won't. If they start losing they are going to use them. If they start winning, they will think we are going to send ours so they will send theirs. And if they have too much time to think that we might launch a first strike, they might send them to keep from losing them along with everything else. We know there won't be any reluctance on their part from a moral standpoint...they believe anything is justifiable for the purpose of destroying us, they know this is their best shot and that they better not blow it. We need to end this as quickly as we can, and a first strike is the way to do it."

"And what do you think of our moral obligation, Benjamin?" Perin asked Gaifen. "Do you think we should act the same as they do and justify anything that will destroy them, even if it saves us?"

"I think we certainly have a moral obligation, sir." Gaifen replied. "But under the circumstances that might best be fulfilled by ending this thing as quickly as possible. It might very well be the option that will cause the least amount of loss and suffering. Things are different now. Without everyone being aligned into East and West camps anymore, there is virtually no chance a limited nuclear engagement will escalate into a wider conflict. Everyone with the big boomers are on the same side. And we should be able to do the job without using anything that would harm too much beyond this theater. Hiroshima and Nagasaki struck a fear into the major powers that has prevented another exchange for generations. Maybe it's time for the same kind of lesson for all the two-bit dictators and expansionists of the world who might somehow get a weapon or two and have no conscience to prevent them from using them. The superpowers hands are tied with these guys, but ours are not."

"And what if we can't locate theirs?" Perin again addressed Gaifen.

"Well, that certainly changes the equation. The strike would still be devastating and should scare some sense into them, but if we can't be sure of destroying their capability then we are really putting ourselves in harm's way. We'd be sure to get some back if we left any."

"Mark, are there any realistic chances of taking them out if they get them in the air?"

"Not much. Everything we have tested or that is available has had poor results at such close range. It will only take four minutes for a missile to get here from Tehran, less from Damascus, and we don't know yet exactly how many they have. It's almost certain one or more will get through."

Perlman had been quiet up to now. "General Engen, what do you think about a first strike, with nukes?"

Mark Engen said nothing for a moment, then began to speak - in a soft, measured tone. "With due respect to Benjamin's comments...I will, for a moment, play the devil's advocate.

I think to be sure we eliminate any chance our enemies might continue their aggression, we will have to use larger warheads and more of them than would allow the damage to be confined only to this area. And of course no one actually knows how wide ranging and long lasting the effects will be. For the same reasons already stated... that they probably see this as do or die, that they will have no moral considerations about throwing everything they have at us...if we are going to launch a first strike it had better be one that does the job. As for our moral obligation...rather than two-bit dictators learning a lesson, a first strike might eliminate the onus of being the first...it could make it easier for countries to start throwing nukes around. When no one thought an exchange of any magnitude was survivable because it would bring in the major powers and worldwide destruction...there was certainly a deterrent. If it can be proven that most of the planet could survive these things, it could make the consequences less daunting. And then, of course, there are the actual catastrophic losses and destruction that will surely occur. Only theirs at best. Both theirs and ours very possibly. Certainly you will all agree that the concept of 'best case' here is still horrendous to contemplate. Hundreds of thousands of people...women and children...suffering gruesome deaths, either immediately or after years of suffering. I think we would be wise to give every other option as much of a chance as we can."

Isaiah Perlman leaned back in his chair, stared at the ceiling and spoke slowly and softly. "Hopefully, we'll have some details on locations soon. We've got to have that."

There is no problem the humans do not seem capable of solving...if their efforts are coordinated and for the right cause. It totally contradicts rational thought - that they contemplate such horrible destruction of their own rather than turning their enormous capabilities to saving their planet. I, Luggalor.

2012

WASHINGTON, D.C.

"Hi Joe, sorry I'm a few minutes late," Sam said, reaching out his hand and smiling warmly. He pulled off the blue, wool, double-breasted overcoat, unwrapped the white scarf from around his neck, and sat down at the corner table in the small, elegant bar.

"Do you think this weather means the end of our outdoor tennis matches for the season?"

"Naw, we'll be able to get a few more in," Joe Chandler answered. "We've got another month before this kind of stuff is here to stay. Which brings me to...it's been over a month since we've played, can you handle a match on Sunday? Alan keeps bitching about us trying to avoid them for a rematch. God he hates to lose. I'm looking forward to kicking their asses again."

"I'll have a Miller Light, please." Sam said as the waitress appeared at the table. And could we have some pretzels?"

"Yeah, I think I can make it Sunday. I need to play or do something other than work. I've been jogging and working out a little, but nothing that's any fun. I've got to get back into playing at least once or twice a week. So how's everything with you?"

"I'm really busy too, as you can imagine," Joe said. "Times like these are hellacious in my business, as they are in yours. Stories and information are coming from all sides, around the clock, and just keeping up with them would be enough of a job even if we didn't have to write and put it all together and get it out once a week. I've got to hit the head, I'll be right back. Encroaching old age has undoubtedly shrunk my bladder. I've only been here two beers longer than you."

Sam watched his old friend disappear down the steps. *Joe looks good. He always looks good.* Sam had known Joe since their undergraduate days at the University of North Carolina. They met in a philosophy class. The professor would sit on the top of his desk and ricochet erasers off the blackboard into a trash can while asking provocative questions they usually couldn't answer...but questions that made for wonderful, beer-soaked conversations later at The Stube. They started hanging out, playing tennis together, and struck up a close friendship that would survive the years through many telephone conversations and sporadic meetings. Joe went to graduate school in journalism at Northwestern, worked his way up through the print media, and is now a senior editor at NEWSWEEK. Since Sam had been in Washington he had seen as much of his friend as he had in the past ten years, and he enjoyed being with him immensely. They always seemed to be on the same page, to understand each other instinctively.

Joe looked at Sam as he sat back down. "What can you tell me about the rumors I'm hearing about more deployments."

"Damn, can't we at least talk about tennis, women, or the virtues of your Saab versus my Rover before you try to coerce me into giving out the secrets of the realm. Besides, you know my tongue doesn't loosen up much with just one beer," Sam said as he motioned for the waitress. "Could we have another round of the same, please."

"Joe, I don't know that I can tell you much you haven't already figured out. The additional deployments are happening. Probably have already started. It looks like we're going to try to get a hell of a lot of people and equipment there real quick."

"What pulled the trigger?"

"It's become obvious that nothing the U.N. is likely to do will slow this thing down. Israel is screaming for more help, and alluding to some pretty grim scenarios if they have to face this alone, considering they've reached the conclusion the Arabs have a fair shot at winning, or at least taking a good bit of their territory."

"What kind of scenarios, Sam.?"

"That's something I can't elaborate on, but then I don't think you really need me to."

"God, Sam, do you think they would really do it?"

"I don't know, but if they won't, the other guys might. The brink...the goddamn, son-of-a-bitchin' brink. Can you believe it? Remember when we were together in New York after the wall came down, were toasting the end of the cold war, and decided we might suddenly have a world out from under the shadow of a nuclear holocaust and we could turn more of our energies and money to saving the environment? But within days of the fall of the Soviet Union there were rumors of Russian scientists and fissionable material on the black market. No good deed...huh? And now this. What the hell happened?"

"But even if it happens," Joe said, "I can't see it spreading beyond the Middle East...there won't be the worldwide devastation, the type of an annihilation we all feared for so long. And I think we knew it ahead of the rumors you mentioned...we knew it from that very conversation in New York. It wasn't that hard to connect the emerging dots. The chances of the big exchange were dramatically reduced, but the odds on a small one had jumped dramatically overnight. Not enough control over any of the components, and those components suddenly floating loose."

"Joe, the people in the area where the damn things land, it's sure as hell going to be annihilation for them, and there's a real good chance a lot of those people will be ours. What's our reaction to that going to be? And then there's the damage from the fallout, nuclear winter...Christ, Joe, you've got to forget I said that. Anyway, you know as well as I that nobody really knows what the overall damage will be."

"What about the Russians?"

"What do you mean?"

"Are they going to give us any help with this thing?

Sam gazed through the window at the bundled, rush hour exodus bending against the cold, raw wind as they moved in double time. He was silent for a few moments, his eyes still toward the window when he did speak. "Everyone is pissed at the Russians because they're using the conflict in Azerbaijan as an excuse not to send anybody. Well, it may be a legitimate excuse, or it may not. They do have a hell of a lot of their people and equipment in there, and it is a real mess. But maybe we should be worrying about something other than whether they will give Israel, and us, any help."

"What are you getting at, Sam?"

"Hypothetical, Joe, all hypothetical."

"I accept that, go on."

"The Russians have been worried for years, back to Khomeini, about the fundamentalists moving across the border...exporting their Islamic fervor. Afghanistan started the serious ticking of the clock. Their economy's still pretty much a wreck...and they're so desperate for money that the oil revenue from Iraq would have to look real good. They've got a large force right there. Once the shooting starts there are a number of excuses they could use to make a move. And then, if the Arabs turn and drop one on them, or just threaten, and there's all that wealth right there..." Sam looked back at Joe, and there was silence between them.

Finally, Joe spoke. "Have you floated this around, Sam? Is this all yours or did you get it somewhere?"

"It's pretty much mine...along with one relatively obscure transmission intercept. Yeah, I've mentioned it to a few people, but I think with everything else they've got to worry about...maybe it's a case of sensory overload. Or maybe it's just a ridiculously farfetched scenario without any possible validity."

"Jesus, Sam, do I ever hope you don't know what the hell you're talking about."

2012

HAIFA, ISRAEL

Suddenly pitched forward, Kabril somehow managed to twist his body just enough to slam his shoulder instead of his face against the wall. The plastic bottle of water spilled over him and began to collect in a pool in the corner of the upturned box. Rolling over so he was on his back, he silently cursed himself for having left it open between sips. He realized he was being off-loaded. Kabril tried to move with complete silence, and without shifting his weight, but knew he must dry the water immediately or it would drain through the hole for the air hose when the crate was tilted back upright. Using the small blanket, he soaked it up as best he could. Suddenly upright again, he reasoned he was now on a lift and would be off the ship in a few minutes. Bracing with his feet and hands against any sudden motion that could cause him to slide, make a sound, or shake the crate, he strained not to move a muscle.

The wait for the feel of being set off the lift was much longer than he expected. His arms and legs ached from being flexed for so long a time, and to avoid the onset of cramps he started releasing one arm and leg at a time, stretching them as much as he could, while continuing to brace himself with the others. Kabril finally relaxed all his limbs together, but kept them positioned against the walls so he could again brace himself at the slightest movement. At last he felt the jolt of the container being set down. Faint voices pierced the box...he knew they must be close because of the insulation. Once more he braced himself.

It had been two hours since the box last moved, and Kabril had heard nothing more. He was beginning to get drowsy, but knew he could not afford to be caught off guard again. Pills had enabled him to sleep much of the time after he was safely aboard the ship and knew he would not be moved again until they arrived. Now he put a pill into his mouth to keep him awake until he was safely through customs and in the truck.

Kabril's thoughts turned to the mission ahead. He, Gamal, Yashim and Uday would be taken to a safe house in east Jerusalem where they would prepare and train the local Palestinians who had been chosen. They were all experienced fighters. There was a large cachet of arms and explosives...everything they would need, including rocket launchers and Tow antitank weapons that had been confiscated from the Israelis.

When the time came, they would launch what would perhaps be the most sacred and important operation since al Fatah, Hamas, Hezbollah, or any or the other groups were formed. They would attempt to take and hold the Wailing Wall and Haram es-Sharif...or as the Jews refer to it, the Temple Mount. The Wall is the Jews most sacred site and the Dome of the Rock and the al-Aqsa Mosque, which are within Haram es-Sharif, are among the most sacred of shrines to all Muslims. If they could succeed in holding the area for a day or two, the outcry might distract the Israelis and play an important role in a successful invasion.

It was without doubt a suicide mission, but Kabril did not care. He was tired of fighting, and by all rights he should have died years before on the beach during the failed raid on Nahariyya. The only survivor, he spent fifteen years in a prison before being exchanged for Israeli soldiers. This was his first major mission since his return, and his request to lead it had been granted as much in payment for his years in captivity as for other considerations. But Kabril knew his experience was critical to the mission, as was that of the other members of the team. Younger, less experienced fighters who could have been used were already in Jerusalem, were not listed, and would not have had to be smuggled in. It was by far the most important mission he had ever been involved with...a mission worthy of dying on. He only regretted he would not live to see the triumphant return of his people to their homeland. A sudden thought of avenging the deaths of his family flashed through his mind, then he remembered that his fire for that had died years ago. *I have probably exacted enough revenge.*

Kabril wondered about the others. In Naples they had each climbed into identical, oversized, industrial ice boxes that were then sealed in crates and loaded onto a British cargo ship bound for the Israeli port of Haifa. There was a hose for air, a small battery operated fan and light, food and water, and the pills. The interior of each box was four feet by four feet and six feet high. There was space to curl up in a fetal position to sleep, and to stand to stretch. The journey south down the Mediterranean coast took three days and had not been so bad. Being able to sleep much of the time made the days and nights run together.

Kabril heard a muffled, whirring noise. The box vibrated...he braced. After a few moments of movement he was sure he was again being lifted and moved. After five minutes or so he sensed the box being lowered, then the movement stopped. Again there were voices, then silence.

Ten hours had passed since the box last moved, or Kabril had heard voices. He knew by his watch it was now 10 p.m., but he also knew that customs sometimes worked through the night if there was cargo backed up. Fighting to keep his eyes open, he kept repeating to himself that he must stay awake. It was becoming difficult.

"These ten are together." The voice was close and clear coming through the air hole, and Kabril knew the instant he came awake that it referred to the ice boxes. He heard the wrenching of the crate being pried open, and reached for the 9mm pistol tucked into his clothing.

What has gone wrong. There is supposed to be someone here, one of our customs agents to be sure none of the four boxes are opened. I will not be taken and go back to a prison camp. He released the safety on the pistol, pointed it at the door, and sat as motionless as he ever had in his life...taking smooth, steady breaths in the stale air.

He felt pressure against the box, heard the sound of metal parting and clinking against the floor, and knew the strapping was being cut away. His heart pounded in his chest.

"Jacob, it is not necessary, I have already opened these two. We must start over here with these. We are behind. Come now, we must hurry."

Kabril waited. He heard nothing more for a few minutes, then voices that were fainter, came from farther away. Placing the gun in his lap, he tilted his head back against the wall and tried to let the tension drain from his body.

Within an hour the box was lifted again. The whirr of an electric motor told him he was on a fork lift, and he thought this time he was probably on the way to the truck. Three taps on the box just minutes earlier told him the person nailing the crate back in place was one of theirs, that they knew they should once again hide the air hole. There were a number of stops and starts, and he kept the pistol ready, just in case. The box suddenly tilted, then was upright again, and there was the clanging of what sounded like a heavy metal door being shut. He heard the screech of the crate being pried off and again the three taps. In another few seconds the door opened.

"I am Hazar. Welcome to Palestine."

2012

WASHINGTON, D.C.

Sam Bradley was alone in the subcommittee hearing room except for a few pages and the TV crews in the back who were busy plugging in wires, drinking coffee, and talking. It occurred to him that the crews always seemed to have a close, jovial camaraderie that made it appear they all work for the same station or network. At least until there was any interviewing to be done. He had planned to be early. This was his first hearing as a member of the armed services committee, and he wanted to have plenty of time to let it soak in, to enjoy the experience.

Sam tried to let every experience soak in...the bad as well as the good. He was never sure if he was better off for it or not. At times he was convinced that people who are able to put disturbing thoughts out of their minds, who could play the ostrich game, compartmentalize with impenetrable walls - spend a larger percentage of their days happier, or at least more content, than he did. At other times he was sure that his willingness to open himself to as much as possible in life made it a much richer experience. Only after a few beers did he always come to the same conclusion...he was sure the latter was true.

Looking across the room again at the cameras, Sam thought of his parents, certain they were already waiting, in front of the TV. He was glad they were alive to see this. The vision of those early years, when their interest in politics and current events had spurred his own interests, was clear and strong. Among relatives around the dinner table, they enjoyed many heated, though always civil, discussions of candidates and ideology. And their son, of course, came to be regarded as quite argumentative.

His thoughts settled on the basic, gentle goodness of his parents, their unwavering dedication to fairness and equality, and how he had come to realize that it was these traits that had been the most positive influence on his life. His mother the teacher, and his father the bookkeeper, had never tried to instill in him the drive and competitiveness that is associated with a black man, or any man for that matter, who graduated from Yale, Harvard Law, started and built a successful public relations company, served on the boards of a few of America's largest corporations, and was now a United States Senator. But it was their beliefs, along with their love and time, that gave him the understanding and ability to take advantage of his opportunities and become successful, without having to sell out his principles.

His mind quickly shifted back to the hearing. It had been a number of years since he served on the board with Robert Quigley. Robert left to take the presidency of H.M.V. Industries a couple of years after his promotion to Executive Vice President and the position on the board. The move had come as a surprise, and had been quite a coup for a man of his age to take over a major division of one of the country's largest defense contractors. Sam and Robert had serious ideological differences back then, and he knew the gap had not narrowed. Sam only hoped that some of the tough questions would still remain when it was his turn. He had a list he imagined Robert would just as soon he had left at home, although he recalled how tough and shrewd an adversary he could be. Neither of them were shrinking violets; there should be some interesting exchanges.

Emerging from his ruminations, he found the room filling with senators, aides, spectators, and the press. He opened his briefing book and had begun to go through some notes when he felt a hand on his shoulder.

"Good morning, Senator Bradley. Congratulations on your election." Robert Quigley had a warm smile on his face.

"Hello, Robert. Thank you."

"Doesn't our knowing each other somehow disqualify you from participating in all this?" Robert asked, with a grin. "I don't guess it really matters though because I'm sure you'll maintain your usual practice of only asking comfortable, non-controversial questions."

Sam studied Robert's face for a moment. It had the easy, confident look and wry smile of someone about to face a familiar, worthy opponent in an important contest. Sam smiled back as he spoke. "Well, when you get to be my age, it's difficult to change your style."

The hearing moved along at what Sam knew was the normal crawl for these events. Many of the questions dealt with background information and highly technical assessments of the armored personnel carrier's specifications, operating procedures, test results, and costs specific to various aspects of the research and development. He was amused by the number of technical, as well as more general questions, that were repeated again and again by each senator as they queried Robert. *Nothing like a good technical grasp of the issue along with a few very pertinent questions...even if they are repeats, to impress the voters back home in front of C-Span.*

Robert looked smaller than his six foot one, wide-shouldered frame as he sat alone at the long table facing the bank of senators behind their ornate, elegant, heavily-paneled enclosure. He was holding his own though, and was as quick, well-prepared and combative as Sam knew he would be.

It was finally Sam's turn to speak. His eyes met Robert's and he began. "Mr. Quigley, it seems there are two issues here and although they are certainly interrelated I would like to address them one at a time. Also, I think my colleagues have done a very admirable job of handling the detailed, technical aspects of this matter, so I will attempt to be somewhat more general with my questions."

Sam continued, "Three years ago the vote was very close when H.M.V. was chosen to produce the POWELL APC, a new high speed, tracked, heavily armored personnel carrier that would replace the MRAP, whose heavy armor has saved many soldier's lives, but lack of speed and maneuverability in rugged terrain or outside of an urban theater is a major problem. There was a great deal of disagreement and competition with the Marine Corp and within branches of the Army itself over whether this was the best choice for a rapid method of moving troops short distances in hostile territory, or if this mission could best be accomplished by a new transport aircraft utilizing stealth and hover technology. The POWELL, of course, won out, and was fast tracked to the extreme. Would you please tell us, Mr. Quigley, what performance and cost projections H.M.V. put before congress at that time that you think were the most instrumental in swinging the vote your way?"

"I'm not sure I understand your question, Senator."

"Let me try again," Sam said. "What do you think were the primary, determining factors in the POWELL APC being selected for production over an aircraft transport?"

"It was demonstrated, without a doubt, that the POWELL was far ahead of the aircraft in meeting or exceeding every primary performance criteria that had been established for its intended mission and operations."

"And these demonstrations were the results of computer enhanced testing and tests with actual prototypes. Is that true, Mr. Quigley?"

"Yes, that is true Senator."

"What role would you say the cost estimates of the POWELL vis a vis the aircraft played in the decision to select the POWELL, Mr. Quigley?"

"They certainly played a role, but I believe the main reason for the selection was, again, that the POWELL did a much better job of meeting the performance criteria."

"The costs estimates for the POWELL were, in fact, twenty percent less than the estimates for the aircraft, were they not, Mr. Quigley?"

"Yes, senator, I believe that is true."

"And they came at a time of economic hardship and a crusade of cost cutting. How do you explain, Mr. Quigley, the fact that your POWELL APC cannot travel as fast, withstand as much enemy fire, or deflect the percentage of a roadside explosive, as was alleged, and demonstrated, during the testing that led to its selection.?"

"The POWELL will operate at each of its projected performance levels after certain adjustments and modifications are made. You can be sure of that, Senator Bradley. Ultra sophisticated, heavy systems of this type commonly need modifications before they become operational."

"Modifications, possibly, Mr. Quigley. But I wouldn't consider increasing a vehicle's speed by twenty-five percent merely an adjustment. And when you add the armor that it appears you are going to have to add to give it the protection you claimed it would have...well, that's probably not going to help make it a threat in the 100 meters either. And rather than have the performance we were promised for less money than the competition, we now have sub par performance with cost overruns that put the POWELL above the projected cost of the aircraft."

Sam paused and leaned forward in his chair, his fingers entwined and holding his chin as he peered at Robert Quigley. "Mr. Quigley, did your company fudge on the performance projections and the costs estimates because you wanted to make sure you got this contract? The evidence seems to be pretty overwhelming."

"As I have stated, there were some irregularities in the initial projections and how they were determined, and those who have been deemed responsible have been terminated from H.M.V. The investigation is still continuing. But again, let me repeat, Senator, the POWELL will meet all the operational criteria as soon as the modifications are completed."

"Well, I certainly hope so, Mr. Quigley, because we might be about to go to war in the desert and need the kind of transport vehicle we were told we were so desperate for, that you could provide, and that we at this moment definitely do not appear to have. "

Sam leaned back in his chair, then spoke again. "I would like to talk about your very generous contributions to the PAC's of certain congressman that voted for the POWELL over what now looks to me may have been a far wiser choice - the aircraft. You maintain that H.M.V. has done nothing technically or legally wrong, and I think it's likely that, in the strict technical or legal sense, you haven't. What I would like to know, Mr. Quigley, is what you think of a system that allows, even encourages, a company such as yours to essentially buy votes for a very large expenditure that may not have been appropriated because of its worth, but rather because of greed and insecurity?"

"First of all, Senator, let me say that I take exception...I vigorously disagree, with any accusations you are making that the POWELL was selected for any reasons other than the proper ones. As for the PAC's, they are one part of the system we use in this country to help fund the enormous costs of a political campaign. I suggest if you think the PAC's are a problem, you should introduce a bill to change the system." Quigley's vise-like control was wavering, betrayed by his voice.

"Mr. Quigley, whether I have a problem with PAC's in theory is not the issue here. What I have a problem with is that your company and its subsidiaries contributed almost one million dollars to four congressmen who changed their votes and in essence put H.M.V. over the top with enough support to insure the POWELL's selection. There must be a better way of doing this. We are constantly wrestling with balancing the budget and searching for much-needed funds for domestic programs. To be successful, we must not spend more money on defense than is necessary, and it is therefore essential that we have honest information and data about weapons, manpower, and the support our military needs in the rapidly changing world we find ourselves facing."

"Yet we have the army, navy and air force each arguing for additional and more expensive weapons and appropriations, not always because of a real need, but often because of competition and a fear of losing their fair share. We have defense contractors who will provide unrealistic figures to back up the military's justification of the programs, and then contribute enough money to influence the votes of the members of congress. And, yes, we have those members of congress who will let themselves be influenced by money and pork barrel politics. Dwight Eisenhower's military industrial complex seems to live on unabated."

"Senator Bradley, our industry operates within the same market system, and utilizes the same dynamics, as any other industry in this country. We compete for business and then must produce a quality product. A failure to do either will prohibit us from being able to attract and maintain a profitable market share."

"There are differences, Mr. Quigley."

"And what are those, sir?"

"Your industry is paid with taxpayer dollars, and in the theater where your product performs...if that product is not the quality you promised it to be, twenty-five young Americans will die a horrible death in a faraway place every time it comes up short."

2012

CHARLESTON, SOUTH CAROLINA

John looked up and back as his count reached four and saw the ball high above him. He strained for an extra burst of speed to keep pace with the tight spiral...*Bubba ain't lost a thing* ...reached, the ball was suddenly in his hands, then tucked it under his arm and covered the twenty remaining yards to the end zone.

"Awright, John baby."

"The man can still catch the long ball."

"Catch the long ball, what about the man that threw the long ball. It was there, baby, right goddamn there." Bubba's high pitched voice brought John memories as he walked back up the field with Tim Graham, who was chasing him on the play.

"John Boy...man, it ain't fair for you to still be in such good shape," Tim complained. "We just ran sixty yards, I'm about to damn die, and you don't even look like you're breathing."

"Yeah, well it ain't like I got a choice. There aren't too many out o'shape Marines. Running around out here without combat boots is a real treat," John Champion replied, as they rejoined the group of men in the middle of the field.

"Deja Vu," Mickey Oliver yelled. "If we coulda had you for the varsity alumni game we coulda really kicked some butt. The rest of us dudes were sucking wind by the second quarter. God I'd love to beat their young asses."

"Speak for yourself, Animal," Bubba tried to sound offended. "The ball was still gettin to where it was supposed to be at the end of the game. There were just a few guys like you that couldn't get to it."

"Right, Bubba, the ball was on the money those two times that your seven-step, seven-minute drop didn't cause you to end up on your fat ass." Mickey laughed while he pointed a finger at Bubba Hoskins. "I coulda taken a phone call between the snap and when you threw it."

"That's all for me. I've got to go"

"Me too. Great game. Let's do it again next Sunday."

"Take it easy. Hey John, if you end up in the desert, kick some raghead butt for me, O.K.?"

"Yeah, man, me too."

George Burnett walked over and put his hand on John's shoulder. "I've got a few beers iced down in the car. Can you hang around for a few minutes and help me with them?"

"Sure, I could use one."

"Be right back."

George was John's best friend in high school, and he had been looking forward to spending some time with him on this trip home. Lying down in the thick grass, John crossed one leg over the other, chewed on the long stalk of a piece of crabgrass, and looked at the graceful, white mare's tails against the deep blue of the autumn sky. *The smell of grass...I love the smell of freshly cut grass... always makes me think of playing football, or baseball, even when I haven't been playing. God I'd love to take this smell with me.*

The familiar, sharp pop of a can being opened signaled George's return. "So, you looked great out there. Man, that's fun." He handed John the can.

"Thanks, yeah, I enjoyed the hell out of it."

"So, how long you gonna to be around for this time? I'm looking forward to us spending some time together."

"I guess I'm not supposed to really tell anybody, but you could always keep a secret. I got a call early this morning. I've got to be back in forty-eight hours. The best bet is we're gonna ship out for Israel."

"Jesus", George said. "You just got here. So when are you going to leave?"

"Tomorrow night. I can take a late flight. I wasn't going to play but I figured I needed it. Exercise is supposed to be good for stress, isn't it? I'll go back and spend tonight and tomorrow with the folks and then take off."

"So what do you think, man. Is this going to be as bad as they're making it sound?"

John hesitated before answering. "It looks like it might. The Arabs have a hell of a lot of men and firepower lined up, and if anybody makes a move it could get real nasty real quick."

"What do you feel like, John? I mean, are you gung ho? Are you anxious to get into it? It seems like a lot of people are."

"My guess is the people who are so gung ho don't have a clue as to what it's really all about. I may not either, but I don't think I'm that anxious to find out. I just didn't do it right. All the hell-raising and partying...man, it just wouldn't have been that hard to stay in school. If I'd just gone out four nights a week instead of seven," John said, finishing his sentence with a small chuckle.

"So how much longer do you have?"

"Not quite two years."

"Do you know what you're going to do when you get out?"

"I'll definitely go back school. I'll have as much of it paid for as I want. Who knows, I might just hang around and get a masters or doctorate. From where I'm sittin now, college is a pretty nice environment. If I ever get back I think I'll stay a while."

"What's going on with you?" John asked his friend.

"Nothing really much different. The two kids, and work, and taking care of the house, I don't have a lot of free time. But that's okay. I can't complain too much. I still get to play an occasional round of golf."

"Yea, occasional my ass. How occasional?"

"Oh, maybe once...sometimes twice a week."

"Let me get my violin, George. Great looking wife with a real brain, two terrific kids, good job with the bank, nice house, golf two times a week, and I'm getting ready to go live in a sand box in a hundred and twenty degree heat, get shot at, and you can't complain too much. Jesus! Have you seen Shawn lately?"

"Yeah, maybe a couple of months ago. She's a features editor now, has a regular column with a byline."

"You think she's still unhappy with that attorney she's going with?"

"I don't know. After what I told you she said a year or so ago, she hasn't said anything about it the last time few times I've seen her. They're still together though."

"Well, I'd better go. I haven't even told my parents I've got to go back early."

They stood and shook hands, holding their grasp and each other's eyes while they spoke.

It was great to see you, John. You take care of yourself, O.K."

"Yeah, I'll try. It was great seeing you too. Maybe when I get home again we'll have time for a few more beers." John broke into an easy smile and hoped his friend understood what he was feeling.

"Is there any place I can write to you?"

"Yeah, my folks will have the address. If you see Shawn, tell her her old buddy sure would appreciate a letter while he's eating beanie weenies in the sand."

"I'll do it."

"Take it easy." John turned and walked to his car.

2012

ASPEN, COLORADO

The van moved slowly through the thin air up the steep, winding, narrow driveway. One final switchback and a contemporary palace filled the windshield. The massive structure's stone, timber and glass architecture was stunning, and matched in impact by the magnificent backdrop of the Maroon Bells, the jagged, alp-like rock peaks that rise above the town of Aspen.

As the vehicle rolled to a stop under the massive port-au-ca-share, they were met by a large man, chest and arm muscles bulging under his tight, long sleeve knit shirt, wearing an earpiece and wire reminiscent of the Secret Service and elite security services. He held a wand that would scan the two men and two women, the van and all its contents.

The security check took at least fifteen minutes, and Li looked away when the wand passed over the metal case containing the set of large, stainless steel carving knives. The metallic clink of the clasps being opened sharpened his focus...on appearing nonchalant...not turning...or moving. He didn't relax until he heard the top of the case fall back into place and the clasp closed.

Enormous wooden beams and curved, decorative timbers formed a spectacular framework for the luxurious leather furniture, Native American rugs, Remington bronzes and western art that filled the main living area. As they walked toward the kitchen Li calculated quickly and guessed two thousand square feet for the space. Then they stepped into another six hundred square feet of industrial strength kitchen, separated from the great room by only two of the massive beams.

It took a number of trips to the van to unload all the containers and coolers of food, alcohol, and cooking utensils. An hour later they were set up and ready to put together the first meal, which would be dinner that evening. Tomorrow there would be three full meals, including an outdoor barbecue, and then only breakfast the following morning. Li removed the cutlery set from the box, slipped the largest knife under his apron when no one was looking, then made sure he had the sharpener and tiny tool in his pocket. Once inside the wash room just off the kitchen, he quickly pried one half of the large, thick black handle away from the stainless steel shaft. Inside the hollowed out piece of ebony was the tiny camera and recorder, no larger than a small, narrow box of promotional matches. Nestled against the steel shaft, it had been safe from the eyes of the giant's security wand. Within seconds the knife's handle had been reassembled, the camera pushed deep inside Li's under shorts, and the knife hidden again for its return to the cutlery set.

The guests started to arrive in the early afternoon, and by 5:00 p.m. were all on the immense timber and slate deck, where cocktails and hors d'ouevres were being served. Considering corporate or private jets had delivered each of them, such a coordinated arrival from so many different locations at the somewhat remote enclave of Aspen was not surprising. It was a crystal clear late summer's afternoon, and as the sun dropped toward the mountain peaks and ridges, a lovely green gold patina flooded the forests and rock faces of the Maroon Bells.

Carlton Abrams was the CEO of one of the country's two largest oil companies, and Bradley Opperman led the other. James Stafford headed up America's only surviving major automobile manufacturer, Mark Silverstein was the CEO of the nation's largest bank, and Gary Shipman helmed the largest insurance conglomerate. Robert Quigley had just been appointed CEO of a major defense contractor, and Steven Gall directed the largest energy conglomerate. Martin Ravenwine headed up one of the nation's largest hedge funds, and owned the palace where these titans of finance and industry were gathered.

As Li passed among the men, taking drink orders, he tried to listen to the individual conversations, but only for himself. They were cordial, mostly social in context. Questions and comments about family, second, third or fourth homes, golf, hunting, fishing, skiing, travel, and other interests and pursuits common to the planet's male elite.

Dinner was served in the large, rustic dining room, at a round table fashioned from an enormous tree trunk that Li guessed could have seated the majority of King Arthur's knights. He had arranged to be the server that would constantly hover around the group, whether to keep all the water and wine glasses filled, or to take orders for anything on the whim of any of those assembled. During the second course, an elegant salad of greens, fruit and exotic nuts, the conversation turned to the purpose of the gathering.

"We're in a mess gentlemen, and we can't miss any chance to have an effect on the outcome of the election. The American free enterprise system cannot stand even one more year of what we've been through for the past twelve." Martin Ravenwine had a booming baritone of a voice, and his eyes flashed with fierce intensity as he spoke. Li's thumb moved deftly and discreetly to activate the tiny camera and recorder hidden in the folds of his starched collar and coat. "All our cherished traditions of individual initiative, entrepreneurship and incentive linked to profitability have been under lethal attack, and if we don't launch an effective counter-offensive it's going to be too late. Global warming, the green revolution, government health care, higher taxes, restrictions on the financial sector, redistribution of wealth...it's going to destroy everything we believe in...everything that allowed each of us to accomplish what we have. Your thoughts, please."

"As the economy has strengthened and gas prices have dropped, there's less interest in alternative fuel sources. We're even seeing signs SUVs, big luxury and muscle cars are getting popular again," James Stafford said. "We will have to keep the

P.R. going with hybrid, electric concept cars and R&D on fuel efficiency and batteries, but with friends in the White House and congress we might be able to make the kind of profits we used to see when everyone wanted something big and brawny, and we could give it to them."

Steven Gall chimed in as he twirled a glass holding a Rothschild vintage Bordeaux. "The taxes to pay for all the R&D and implementation of alternate energy, even the national grid that gets so much attention…well, the reality of the tax increases and their effect on Joe-Bag-O-Doughnuts cash flow is sinking in. I agree. If we can get the right guy in the White House and a majority in one or both houses, the time is right to turn back the clock to a better business environment and see significant profits again,"

Ravenwine's voice again filled the room. "We can get this done if we spend tonight and tomorrow exploring our best options. As we had hoped, and suspected, after the recession's witch hunt for CEOs and money guys like me, we're beginning to see some loosening of the restrictions and structure that made so much political hay. The folks who know how the world really works and how critical reward is to risk have renewed influence. The rain delay could be over if we can orchestrate this. If we can find the right candidate…make sure we get enough money to them…and put together the strategy and ads that will turn people against this goddamned liberal agenda…" His intensity was constant, fierce, even though his body language was relaxed as he leaned back in his chair with his legs crossed.

"Credit markets aren't getting the scrutiny they were. The tide does seem to be changing toward less protection for investors and more chances to make money for those who lend it, sell it, or bet on it. There's an excitement building in the banking industry for potential profits and compensation that hasn't been there for a while." Mark Silverstein spoke in a soft, authoritative voice. "We all know when things get better, time goes by, people forget.

Become risk takers again. We've got to continue loosening the restrictions, the oversight, that inhibits the chance for big time profits and compensation that has always driven our system...and has been responsible for the incredible growth and success of the Republic in the relative heartbeat of time comprising our history."

"The drug and insurance industries would share your optimism if we can get the next installment of health care reform defeated. They got too much last time, and if everyone has guaranteed coverage and the government is running a good part of it, we're in real trouble. I'll do all I can to help elect anyone who will put the health care industry back in the hands of the market and the private sector," Gary Shipman said, joining the freewheeling discussion. "Reforms have been killing profitability."

Ravenwine's bright blue eyes came to rest on Robert Quigley, seated on the opposite side of the table. "Robert, do you think you could start building profitable weapons systems again if we end up with a defense secretary who doesn't always question how much the military really needs what it asks for?"

"I was hoping I could sit quietly and listen this evening...so I could be assured of staying and enjoying the company and fantastic food for another day. I'm going to be the devil's advocate in this discussion." As Quigley finished his sentence, Li sensed all eyes around the table narrowed at once.

"I like to make money for myself and our stockholders as much as any of you, but I haven't heard one mention of the larger, critical problems we face, and what those of us around this table can do to affect solutions. Just the same concerns with profits and compensation. Given our power and profiles, we're in a position, gentlemen, to affect changes that will do some real good in a world that desperately needs it. And the irony – after we've had to bite the bullet for a while during the transition – we'll be back to substantial profits with new products and technologies, and they will be sustainable. Not temporary...until the price of oil rises and we're forced to once again to confront the same problems we never put our best efforts into solving."

"I'm listening, Robert. Go on," James Stafford spoke with a flat, hard voice.

"Jim, there's no industry that could lead by example better than yours. You're right, the American people's infatuation with cars and status means that many of them will buy vehicles they can't afford and use gas we shouldn't be burning. And your profits will rise. But only for a time. Throwing all your weight and resources behind developing batteries and natural gas systems that would relieve our dependence on oil and all the problems that entails… and if you are first, with the best electric cars…then that hallowed American tradition of innovative and quality products will allow you to be highly profitable…well into the future. There are tremendous profits to be realized in the alternate energy industry. It's the next great commercial revolution…like the computer industry…and the online industry. It may offer more opportunity than either. Trillions of dollars in profits. We just have to bite the bullet for a while through a transition in the goals we set for running our businesses."

"And I suppose you're going to tell us what these new goals should be." Ravenwine's voice now had an edge.

"Simple in principal. The big issues…the problems that are a fact…environmental degradation, dependence on foreign oil, poverty, health care…we all know what they are. If our decisions regarding the direction our companies take…the products and services we bring to the market…are informed as much by how they will contribute to solutions to these problems as they are by profitability…we'll make a tremendous contribution outside of the bottom line. We don't need government to beat the free enterprise system out of enormous profit potential by taking on the innovation and new technology associated with these emerging markets. We should be solving these problems, and making a tidy profit in the balance. But it will require us to think about the common good as much as profits…whatever our real motivation.

This devil's advocate isn't going to harp on moral responsibility. Just a longer vision that will assure sustainable profits...and a better world...for our grandchildren."

"And what brought on this sea-change in your thinking, Robert? We've talked on a number of occasions, and I don't remember this kind of philanthropic, world view."

"Not only philanthropy, Martin. I'm talking about using the best minds and the best economic system in the world to solve the world's major problems. With the same profit incentive that has made this country the only surviving superpower. Sure, I've been thinking for some time that I want to be known for something other than making money and questionable products, and how critical it is to find solutions to the major issues. And I finally realized that using my position to help and making money need not be exclusive of each other...that I can be most effective if I do both."

"What you're proposing means years of lower profits, and dividends, and compensation," Carlton Abrams said, joining the conversation for the first time. "And even higher taxes."

"True. But we're talking about relative numbers. Stockholders will have to be educated to the necessity and potential of contributing to the common good while at the same time planning for sustained growth and profits well into the future. And we'll all have to settle for a bit less. Higher taxes are a fact if we're to pay what's needed for solutions while keeping the deficit out of the stratosphere, but if we can ever get a handle on wasteful spending and political pork, they won't be have to be that much higher. If taxes buy real value, and people are educated as to what's needed, they will accept the cost," Robert said as he shifted his glance to Ravenwine. "Martin, if you concentrate your lending and investments on innovative companies and products in the alternative energy industry, you may only make $50 million for a few years instead of $100 million...but you'll make $50 million." The money manager did not look amused. Robert smiled broadly.

"Come on…we can all get by on a bit less through the transition. Maybe even forever…if we're really doing some good."

"Epiphany comes to mind here. Is there anything that put you over the edge on this?" Gary Shipman's voice was the first that had an open edge of sarcasm.

"The kids I suppose. I've got two very bright college students. They keep asking me why anything that could help with solutions to our major problems seems to be anathema to the business community and politicians known for supporting business leaders. They keep telling me that paying more taxes if it's necessary to right the ship…cutting profits in the short run if it will help… shouldn't piss off so many capitalists. When your kids tell you that your contributions to the world community and its issues are as important as those to yourself and your company…how are you going to argue?"

Robert continued. "My daughter gave me a quote I can't get out of my mind. It's from the philosopher Theodor Adorno. "The conversion of all questions of truth into questions of power…has attacked the very heart of the distinction between true and false."

The main course, featuring bison steaks and king crab, was served. Their was initial silence around the table, then a forced conversation about the local ranch that provided the thick slabs of grilled buffalo that were on their plates. Robert knew his words elicited no support, only condemnation. *Might be a long couple of days.*

Even the brightest humans can be so stubborn…so intractable in their views. Even if the truth is right in front of them. The filters on their lens prejudice so many of their thoughts. I, Luggalor.

2012

LAS VEGAS, NEVADA

"And now it gives me the greatest pleasure imaginable to introduce to you the most Honorable Representative to the United States Congress, our own Jennifer Stark Baker."

The applause erupted, engulfed her, and the thrill of its stunning intensity coursed like a charge through her body. Shrill whistles and screams of 'yeah' and 'all riiight' pierced the din. It went on and on...no one seemed interested in sitting down. She waved and smiled, finally moved the few steps to the podium and started to adjust the microphone, then heard the rhythmic stomping of feet and. "Jen ni fer...Jen ni fer...Jen ni fer." Tears welled in her eyes. Stepping back, she started waving again, buying time to compose herself, but also to take in and revel in each moment of the scene.

After the applause finally subsided, she stepped forward and began to speak, "Thank you."

It began again. "Jen ni fer...Je ni fer." She smiled broadly and shook her head. After a few more moments of the chant she tried again. "Please, please, you are much too kind. Thank you from the bottom of my heart."

Again the crowd erupted, but this time their volume quickly subsided...then became quiet enough for her to start. "President Holland, members of the executive council and esteemed members of the world's most important profession..." She was interrupted by another deafening roar that seemed louder than anything she had heard so far. Again she waited.

"I cannot possibly express to you what a thrill it is for me to stand here before you. There is no doubt in my mind that each and every one of you are what made the difference, that you are the real reason I am now a member of the United States Congress, and I'm here to thank you and tell you this is one congresswoman who's not going to let you down." More applause…whistles… applause.

"Teaching…the world's most important profession. And why? It's quite simple, really. Because educating is the world's most important task. I believe this with all my heart and I want to talk tonight about what I must do…and what you must do…to enable our profession to live up to its enormous promise, and the responsibilities inherent in that promise."

"Teaching has always been crucially important in the development of America's most important resource…the same resource that is the most important for each and every nation…each and every group of people on earth…their children. However, with the disintegration of the traditional family unit in segments of our society, widespread poverty, the availability and allure of drugs and their profits and the violence that surrounds this horrid industry, the assimilation of an ever increasing number of non-English speaking immigrants, and the mounting pressures on all our children to be successful in a world that becomes more competitive daily…I say to you that there can be no doubt that teaching is now more important than ever…in this country as well as throughout the world. And by virtue of its importance it should no longer be viewed as a mere job…it must be viewed as a mission, a quest, a sacred crusade." Again there was loud applause and a few people jumped to their feet.

"To meet the ever-growing list of responsibilities that society and its ills are now thrusting upon our profession, to ensure that the promise of our young people and our world will not be wasted…we will need help in two areas."

"Each of you and every new teacher who will join our ranks in the years to come must be diligent, uncompromising, relentless…in your pursuit of excellence in each of your ever-increasing list of responsibilities to your students. The second area we need help in is from people like myself, and ultimately the taxpayer, who also votes. We simply must obtain the resources to provide the training, facilities, materials, and yes...the compensation for you...that is necessary and consistent with your responsibilities and status as the world's most important professionals."

The applause started again, rose in a crescendo, and continued....with more whistles and 'all riiights'.

"I keep mentioning your growing list of responsibilities. I would like to address those for a moment. We all know that learning and its coxswain, motivation, should start in the home. If it is started and nurtured in the right way at home, there is little you can do as teachers that can equal the positive impact an involved parent and family can have on a student's desire and ability to learn. The problem is, large numbers kids are coming from homes where no one is there to start and nurture the learning process...or if someone is there, they are often too busy chasing their own successes...or working like slaves to provide the basics for subsistence. You'll have to take over this job as best you can for many students. You'll have to teach them the worth and beauty of knowledge...then motivate them to pursue it...if you are to have success in helping them attain it. And you'll have to figure out how to keep them away from the frightening consequences of drugs...irresponsible sex...and the other temptations and peer group pressures they all face to one degree or another. In many cases you'll have to be a parent, role model, sociologist and psychologist...as well as a teacher. Immigrants and those with learning disabilities, as well as those who are gifted...will need even more of your help. You must be adept at using different strategies to meet the needs of this very diverse group of students. You'll have to do whatever it takes to help a dyslexic child from a broken home and the ghetto achieve his significant potential...as well as prepare the student capable of becoming a microbiologist and curing the world's hunger problems to achieve hers. This may seem too much to ask...but you're truly our last best hope."

"Of course, many of you already wear these different hats, and play these different roles...but you'll have to do more. And to prepare yourselves to do more you should take every course and seminar you can...have every discussion possible with your colleagues...read everything you can lay your hands on that might help you. You must be relentless in your pursuit of the tools you need and their application to this task you must succeed in."

"And if all that doesn't sound like too much to handle...there are other crucially important responsibilities you must bear. You must educate parents and taxpayers to the importance of quality education...what it costs...and the necessity of paying for it. And of course we must all be held accountable. If we cannot motivate...and teach...to the highest standards...with verifiable results...we must step aside in favor of those who can." Limited applause...even a few muted boos. Jennifer waited, scanned the room. "If we receive the resources we need to succeed...and are compensated at the level we should be...we must allow ourselves to be held accountable." Applause...but still muted.

"Now for my responsibilities...and my promise that I will not let you down. I will carry the message of our mission to every level of government and through every level of educational administration... from local and state boards, to local and state governments, to the Congress of the United States, the Department of Education and to the President himself. I will carry the message in speeches, and articles, and interviews, and I will introduce legislation and amendments and fight for appropriations."

"And what will my message be and what will I fight for? It will be that quality education is the only hope we have for addressing the staggering challenges we face every day in our country and throughout the world. It will be that we need to make important decisions...decisions about the best curriculums, the best teaching methods, the best learning environments to ensure that each and every child...regardless of race, color, nationality, social status or learning ability...not only has the opportunity, but is motivated to take advantage of that opportunity...to be everything they are capable of being, and in turn help our world become everything it should be."

The applause from the audience was immediately at full cry. Jennifer waited until it subsided, but had not stopped, and then continued, her voice rising above it all. "My message will be that we must have the money to pay for designing and implementing the curriculums we need...that we must have the money to pay for new schools and the renovation of old ones, and for the materials that will help us create this fertile learning environment for every one of our children. That we must have the money to hire, train, and keep in this profession the best our society produces....because this most important of tasks requires nothing less than the best."

The applause was again thunderous...and the chants began. "Jen ni fer....Jen ni fer." Again she waited. When she spoke she was practically screaming to be heard over the crowd. "You are members of the world's most important profession...you are undertaking the world's most important mission...you are crusaders of the highest order...and you deserve to have the resources you need and be paid accordingly. Be..." The explosion of their sounds of approval washed over her but she only hesitated for a moment. "Be relentless in your mission as I will be in mine, and I promise you will have what you need and you will be rewarded." She raised her arms over her head and smiled, and tears slid down her cheeks.

Laying her head back against the headrest, Jennifer closed her eyes. She was not ready to try to sleep just yet, but was a little weary of talking, or rather listening, to Ida Haskins, the sprightly, charming, kindly ball of energy of eighty-one in the seat next to her, who had just recited her whole life story as well as those of her children and her favorite granddaughter, whom she had just spent the week with in Disneyland. It took a couple of forays into the physical maladies of her late husband, without any response or acknowledgment from Jennifer, before she got the hint. Or perhaps Ida had just run too low on saliva to lubricate her tongue. Jennifer relished the silence when it finally came, and tried to relax and let the tension flow from her body. Her thoughts turned inward. *Forty one years old...married, although not too well at the present...beautiful, wonderful six-year-old son that's the love and pride of my life...representative to the United States Congress...returning from a speech that resulted in overwhelming acclaim from my peers and the media. Healthy... in pretty good shape...not too bad...but I need to work on the marriage, or get another one, or do without. I'll have six days at home before the trip to Bangladesh. Ten days altogether on that adventure. God, I'm not looking forward to it. I don't want to leave Cory again so soon. But then I should be home for a month or more except for a few speeches that I can give without staying overnight.* The image that filled Jennifer's mind brought her great pleasure - Cory's face breaking into that amazing smile whenever she walked through the door.

I am always stunned to see how magnificent the humans can be when they devote their extraordinary minds and skills to the right issues, to the common good. But why do so many concentrate all their resources on themselves, or the wrong endeavors? I, Luggalor.

Jennifer's thoughts turned to the upcoming trip. *Bangladesh will be a real bummer. I'm only going because of my low rank on the committee. I'm certainly concerned enough, but I just don't have the stomach for the kind of suffering I'll see. Some people need to see it to know it's there, its magnitude. I don't and it will depress me for a long time. As it should. Bangladesh is our worst nightmare come true... early. Well, the Middle East ranks up there at the moment. Just a different type of nightmare. Not like those I used to have where I die a horrible death....but the one where my parents do and I'm forced to watch. Is one worse than the other? The trip might be cancelled if the Israeli situation gets worse...not something to hope for...there's no lesser of the two evils this time.*

143

Environmentalists and the scientific community have been predicting various stages and effects of global warming for a long time. Bangladesh proves once and for all they were all off - on the conservative side. They thought the temperature rise in fifty years could cause the polar ice to melt enough to raise sea levels to dangerous levels. It has taken only twenty, some beaches and condos are already in jeopardy, and new marshland is lapping at shopping centers. But our problems pale next to those of Bangladesh. Many people think global warming causes more heat and less rain and in certain areas of the world that's exactly what's happening. Bangladesh, however, has the opposite problem. There's much more rain and runoff from the Himalayas than before, and the severe and constant flooding it causes, along with the loss of one-sixth of their land to the rising sea, has wreaked havoc with what was at best a primitive and inefficient agricultural industry. Acid rain caused more widespread damage earlier than predicted, and its effects are magnified there because of the sea level and flooding situation. Throw in one of the world's fastest growing populations of not just dirt poor but starving people, displaced into horrid, squalid, disease ridden camps...a recent, full blown regional AIDS epidemic...a corrupt government and a terrorist oriented insurgency, both of which keep food and medical relief away from the millions who desperately need it...it's a microcosm of the world's worst problems. And a harbinger of what's to come, in more places and likely with more devastating circumstances...as inconceivable as that now seems. Guilt. I should feel guilt for feeling so good a minute ago when the world is going to hell in a hand basket. But I understand that irony, how that works...how I can, and have to, view the two as separate entities at times...many times. Or it's just too depressing.
Jennifer reached for the in-flight magazine and turned to the listing of audio programs. Country Sounds; The Best of Rock; An Evening of Comedy; Beautiful Bach, Fugue in C Major; Broadway Classics; Let's try Broadway. Plugging her earphone set in to the armrest, she turned the knob to channel six.

I started to leave Jennifer, but the sound coming through her earphones kept me with her. Elegant, soothing tones mesmerized me. I had not heard a Bach fugue since the last time I was on planet 1003, over eight complete revolutions of the source star ago, so I went to the lens of a young man across the aisle that had his earphones on.

"Ha Haaaaaaa...Haaaa Haaa." A male voice blasted through the earphones. The young man's mind was filled with vivid images of his interpretation of the story coming through the earphones. Nothing else broke through to his conscience thought. His eyes remained closed, he kept laughing...roaring now, oblivious to all those around him.

Leaving the laugher, I tried the lens of a girl in a military uniform two rows back. She was madly tapping her hands against the armrests and what was coming through her earphones was definitely not a Bach Fugue.

In my invisible form, I placed myself in an empty seat. Glancing around at the different humans I decided to try the lens of a man with glasses and long hair, whose sight mechanisms were fixed on a book. The wondrous sounds of the Fugue in C major again captivated me, and I decided to stay with this human, but concentrate on my own thoughts

This trip back to planet 1003 has so far been a qualified success. The humans are as fascinating as ever, and now the Council, due to the insights gained from my visits using the lenses, has a direct line of sight into the reasons behind the innumerable variations of their thoughts and actions. I have been more intrigued than ever by their behavior since developing an understanding of the thought processes that caused each of them to think and function the way they do.

But understanding the reasons for their behavior was only half of the equation. The other half, and the reason the council sent me back for a third visit, was to try to determine if anything can be done to change the destructive thoughts and actions that are so prevalent, and such a serious threat to 1003. From what I have seen in the short time I have been back, the fate of the planet and all its life forms are more in doubt now than when I was last here...and the prognosis was not good then. And of course I must still find The Wise One. When my prior visit was cut short due to the emergency on Planet 3683, I left before finding The Wise One.

The Wise One...I wonder when I will receive the instructions to enable me to find The Wise One. The Council has always known about the existence of The Wise One. I wonder if The Wise One will have the answers.

The human listening to the Fugue in C major fell asleep and the music kept repeating. I was transfixed by the magical, sublime sounds until a man's voice interrupted, "Ladies and gentlemen, we are beginning our final approach." I, Luggalor.

2012

JUDEAN DESERT, ISRAEL

"Gin!" John shouted, slapping his cards, face up and arranged by suits, onto the camouflaged, nylon liner spread out on the sand. "That's ten bills, ten buckeroos, Cristol. You better quit and go clean your weapon again before I take everything you own."

"I'm not worried, Sergeant Champion. Besides, what the hell do I need money for out here anyway. If I lose it all, I'm confident you'll take pity on me and buy my beer, just like I'm going to do for you after I finish my comeback and get my money and all of yours and all of Jones's that you won yesterday."

"All right, Cristol, don't say I didn't warn you. Just trying to look out for you, you know. Got to take care of all my guys."

John thought about Private Nathan Cristol as he gathered in the cards and began to shuffle. He liked the kid a lot. Sure didn't look like your typical Marine...didn't act like one either. Short with a small frame, but unlike so many short guys in the Corp, he didn't have that 'Napoleonic, can't-wait-to-take-on-anything-that-moves-to-prove-I'm-a-tough-guy' complex. He was tough all right, but in a different way. Cristol had never been quite able to hide his fear when he was scared. Many times he didn't try...but he always did whatever he had to do, scared or not, and John appreciated and respected the hell out of that. He was honest...not only with what he said and did, but with his feelings...and that kind of honesty seemed practically nonexistent in this group of trained killers that John was convinced had one of the highest ratios of insecure, confused, macho-wannabees in existence. John dealt, effortlessly, quickly spinning each card to rest on top of the previous one...in front of the private, then to himself, then to the private.

"Hey sergeant, I got you this time. Not a prayer, not one lousy prayer do you have. These are the cards that will turn the tide, the beginning of the end for you. You've had it."

John recalled wondering, when Cristol first came into the platoon, what led him to the Marines. After they had talked a few times, he asked, and Cristol explained that he had been in some trouble with drugs, dropped out of school, and his family had cut him off. He reached a low point and decided the best way to make significant changes was to do something he knew would be hard and out of character for him, but would teach him some discipline and get him straightened out as quickly as possible. He had laughingly told John it all would have worked out great if he could have just left the Marines as soon as he had his head back on straight...which he said took about two weeks of boot camp.

John knew Cristol was scared now, as they all were. But he was confident he could count on him once the shooting started...as much as he thought he could count on any of them, including himself. And Cristol was Jewish. John sensed he was not very religious, but thought it must mean something extra to him...being over here. A deep, serious thinker. It must effect him.

John took a chance and discarded one of his two sixes to draw to the seven, eight and nine for a straight. He wasn't counting cards as he usually did, but was pretty sure he saw one six come across. He drew the ten of hearts and nonchalantly tossed them face up. "Hell of a comeback, Cristol. Man, aren't you ever going to learn?"

His body jerked over for what must have been the twentieth time during the long hours John had been trying to fall asleep. Outside the camouflage and tent to get as much air as possible, he still sweated like a hog. *These guys who were here a couple of months ago and keep talking about it being cool now compared to then, what the hell does it matter...ninety degrees at night, a hundred and fifteen during the day....Jesus. I'll look for shooting stars....God, I'll never forget the stars here, incredible. Seems like a lot of the paintings of the night sky in this part of the world are filled with stars or a huge moon, or both.   Talk about realism...they're zillions of them, and the cloud of the Milky Way is so clear.*

Will this be the night?   Everybody thinks it's got to be real soon. The moon's down, and a night attack would definitely favor us... the blacker the better.... so they probably won't come now. They'll wait until there's more light or probably attack during the day. I wonder if the Israeli's would attack and not even tell us dumb grunts out here in the sand. Probably not, but it's possible. It'll be all planes and long range artillery and missiles at first anyway.   Jesus, I still shiver every time I think about it.   You'd think it would ease up after you've thought about it hundreds of times.   What will it really be like?   I've read and listened, but I know there's nothing I can imagine that's going to be like the real thing. How the hell did I end up in this stinking desert, completely exposed except for some sand bags and camouflage, with half a million holy-war-crazed Jew-hating Arabs just a few miles away with tanks, guns, missiles, chemical, even nuclear weapons, frothing at the mouth to roll right over us and get the hell to Jerusalem.

Panic suddenly seized him...every muscle, every fiber in his body seemed to constrict.   It usually came like this...quickly, without warning. The familiar sense of desperation followed. It was really going to happen...there's nothing that could help him...everything was beyond his control.   *Have to think of something else...think of something else until the time comes, then just do my job. That's all I can do. They won't drop anything big or chemical or nuclear on Jerusalem or this close to it. Why the hell would they do that? That's their prize, what they're doing this for, and they've got too many people there to destroy it. It makes more sense for them to wipe out everything else and then march right through here and right on in. Come on, dammit, think about something else...sex. Shawn, naked in...*

A screeching blast of noise and a shock wave exploded through

149

him, and instantly John was on one knee, reaching for his rifle, as the thunder of two Israeli fighters flying night patrol just above passed and continued to erupt along their northbound heading. He leaned on his rifle for a moment, still on one knee, and dropped his head. *God, please help me, please keep me safe. Please keep my men safe. Please keep this horrible thing from happening. They're so many lives, innocent lives. Please don't let it happen.*

2012

TEL AVIV, ISRAEL

General Mark Engen was finishing breakfast with his wife Ruth, and would soon leave for a day of meetings in the situation room before going back into the field...unless the schedule was disrupted. It had been four days since he was last home, and he wished more than anything he could stay, but since he could not, he was anxious to leave. Conversation between them was awkward. There were so many things he would have liked to say and, he suspected, she would have liked to say....but they either could not or would not.

Zack, his nine year old son, and Anna, who was six, walked into the dining room with their books. "Daddy, when are you coming home again?" his daughter asked.

"Soon. I'll call you both tonight, or if I don't have a chance, then tomorrow. Have a good day at school and good luck again on your recital. And Zack, good luck on your match." He tried to act reassuring, normal, and show none of his fear and despair. He wanted so badly to hug each of them, to hold them for a long time. But he knew they would sense something. And he might fall apart. His two children turned and left. *And now another good-bye for Ruth. This could be the end of it.* Feeling the emotion coming, Mark knew he must walk through the door as quickly as possible and into the car waiting for him at the curb so he could put his mind away from his family.

"I'll call and let you know when I'll be back. Hopefully, it will only be a couple of more days. Wish Zack good luck again in his match and Anna the same with her recital." Mark grabbed his hat and coat, moved to Ruth, kissed her quickly on the lips and immediately turned to leave, glancing at his watch and acting hurried so he did not have to see her eyes or hear the sorrow in her voice.

"Good morning, General."

"Good morning, Peter, thank you," Mark said, climbing into the back seat of the car as his driver held the door open for him. Mark leaned back into the corner of the seat and thought ahead to the upcoming meetings, especially the intelligence briefing. The Mossad supposedly pinpointed most of the weapons, and he was anxious to find out what the situation was and everyone's thoughts on the options. He wondered if he would find out whether the enemy knew they now have everything, or at least most of it, targeted. *A critical issue in this insane game.*

The intelligence briefing was the first thing on the agenda and it didn't take long. There were seven known nuclear warheads, with five located amidst the heaviest defensive positions in and around Tehran and Damascus, and the other two around Baghdad. Two strong opinions favored going ahead with a nuclear first strike when Mark was called upon for his views on what they now know, and what they should do.

"I think we must wait. They should have the capability to tell when we have launched, and if they do, they will certainly fire all of theirs. If we do wait and they launch first, we will know it immediately and answer. Incredible devastation on both sides in both cases. If we wait, or just launch a conventional strike, there are two possible scenarios that would not result in a nuclear exchange. They might not attack. With the increased American involvement and world condemnation, they just might decide it is too risky. They certainly know that if they lose this time, with the stakes they have put on the table, their power will be gone for generations. If they do attack without the nukes, and we retaliate in kind, or if we mount a conventional attack, there is still the chance the nuclear option would not be used, or that we might be able to take it out. They know we have more than they do and ours are more accurate, and then there is the half life of the U-235...the precise and diligent monitoring of the detonation devices that we are pretty sure is necessary. Theirs might not work and they might know it, in which case it does not make a great deal of sense for them to guarantee their destruction on only a chance they could do major damage to us. You have all heard this argument from me before. It just seems the only chance we have to avoid a doomsday scenario is to wait until they make a move, or to strike with the conventional stuff. Any chance to avoid annihilation and loosing this on the world is more than worth it in my opinion."

Benjamin Gaifen was quick to reply. "But Mark, your argument actually supports a nuclear strike. If they are so afraid of losing, then it seems clear they are going to shoot them either at the beginning or whenever they think they might be starting to lose. If they never start losing, then we are doomed anyway. And I'm not so sure they can tell when we have launched or that their targeting systems are that accurate. There are a lot of unknowns about their ability to really hit us."

Mark started to respond to Gaifen about the meaning of his last statement and the benefits of letting an enemy know their warheads are targeted, but he decided to wait. He knew what would happen. *It's all so diabolical. Each argument can be turned to circle and support the opposing view, and all roads seem to lead to an unthinkable tragedy. The best hope for restraint is with the politicians. Why must the military always want to blow everything away?*

2012

IRAN

"Allah Akbar!"

"Allah Akbar!"

"Death to the Zionists!"

"Death to the Zionists!"

"Death to America!"

"Death to America!"

"Slaughter the infidels!"

"Slaughter the Infidels!"

"Allah Akbar!"

"Allah Akbar!"

The cries erupted from the throats of 20,000 men, and fired Saleh's emotions to a feverish pitch as he raised the AK47 over his head and screamed, louder and louder, with the cadence.

"Death to the Zionists!

"Death to America!"

"Death to America!"

He touched the gold key hanging from the chain around his neck. Personally blessed by the Iman, it assured his place in heaven should he die a martyr in the holy war. Every one of his twenty thousand comrades had an identical key. Saleh had never been so excited, and he screamed so loud and hard that he suddenly had trouble catching a breath, and started to gasp. He was silent for a moment, until his breathing was easier. He hoped no one had noticed. Screaming again, he tried to make his voice rise above the others. A feeling of enormous pride rolled over him. *I am a man. I am blessed by the Iman and Allah. I am a warrior...and I will drive the hated enemy from the sacred land.*

After what seemed like hours, the officers requested quiet and Saleh, with the others, returned to attention, exhausted and aching from waving his rifle in the air for so long. He had screamed the same words and threats against the enemy in training every day. But never with so many men, and never with so much feeling.

Standing there awaiting orders, he thought of his family. They would be very proud if they could see him now, and they would be very proud of him after the war. If he lives and returns home he will be welcomed and treated as a hero. If he dies he will be a martyr, and there is no greater honor than that. His father, the other men in his family and his officers were right. It would be a great privilege to be able to die for so holy and sacred a cause. Many never have the opportunity.

He turned and marched off with his company for more drills. Saleh hoped they would be the first to attack, and that it would be soon.

2012

DHAKA, BANGLADESH

The stench was overpowering as they entered the refugee camp. Standing water, laced with raw sewage, was everywhere, and Jennifer felt herself begin to wretch. Swallowing hard, she took a deep breath. *God, thank God, this is the last one.* A few more hours, one more press conference, and they would be back at the hotel, and then tomorrow, on their way home. She had seen enough...far more than enough, to understand the enormity of this country's desperation and tragedy, and the implications for the world if something cannot be done to slow and eliminate the causes.

The reporter, photographer, Jennifer, and the two other congressmen were ushered by their guide into a crude lean-to where ten to fifteen children huddled around three women, one of whom was very old. The guide told them the old woman was the only person over sixty still alive in the camp. She looked ninety. All emaciated, the children had the swollen bellies and huge, empty eyes she had come to expect and dread at every stop. One of the women lifted a small child and handed her to Jennifer. Tears filled her eyes, as they always did. She could never get used to this. She hated it...hated the world for it...sometimes wanted to hate God for it. It was unfathomable. She tried not to listen as the guide translated what the mother was saying to her. Didn't he know if there was any way for her to take this child...all these poor, innocent, doomed children, that she would? Couldn't he see that hearing the pleading ripped her heart out?

They were moving slowly through the camp when a man walked hurriedly up to the guide. The two turned their backs toward the group and had a brief, animated conversation before the stranger left, again moving in double time.

"There has been a change in the schedule," the guide said, "We are to leave and go back to the hotel now."

Jennifer gazed out the window of the bus as they bounced and lurched along the heavily rutted road back to town, but she saw little while lost in her thoughts. It had been even worse than she imagined. *So much of the land taken by the sea, with towns now standing in salt water. And water everywhere else to ruin the cotton and what precious little other agriculture and subsistence crops there are. It never stops raining. And then there are the Shanti Bahini, the rebels, who keep relief efforts from getting to the millions dying of starvation, and the government, more intent on fighting the rebels and preserving a system of rampart corruption than saving its people.*

Seventy-four people had come on this fact-finding trip. Thirteen members of congress, twenty two members of the scientific community, assorted aids, agency officials, medical personnel, translators, photographers, and the press. Jennifer could not imagine how any of them, even the most jaded and skeptical, considering what they had seen, could not now be terrified by the thought of what is happening to the planet. The environmentalists, scientists and other doomsayers have been vindicated, although even they were far from accurate with their predictions of the time it would take these devastating effects of the greenhouse and global warming to come to pass, and their magnitude. The consensus seemed to be that a critical mass was reached at some point in the last few years. Before that apocalyptic threshold was passed, the greenhouse effects crept slowly, sometimes almost imperceptibly. It was as if they were moving up a long, slight, uphill grade. Once at the crest, the road turned downward, and steeply, and the acceleration was now frightening. Somehow the world would have to be convinced that we must act, with whatever it takes, if there is to be any hope.

Filing slowly into the hotel, Jennifer noticed a large contingent of the group standing, milling around in the lobby. It appeared everyone had been recalled from their various, gruesome outings and inspections, and there seemed to be an air of excitement. After the long ride, she had an aching need to go into the bathroom off the lobby, and decided to wait until she returned to find out what was going on.

When she stepped back into the hall she almost ran into Li as he was going into the men's room.

"Unbelievable, Jennifer, unbelievable." Li said, shaking his head.

"What Li...what's going on?"

"You haven't heard? That depression organized and strengthened dramatically overnight, and was declared a cyclone this morning. The predictions are it will be major storm, with catastrophic damage." A hint of a pained smile crossed Li's face. "As if there could be any other kind around here ever again. Anyway, it's headed right down the middle of the Bay of Bengal towards us, and they are trying to get us out of here tonight. There's supposed to be a briefing as soon as everyone gets back. I'm thinking about staying, but please don't tell anyone."

Jennifer studied her new friend for a moment, then asked a question she was sure she already knew the answer to. "Why do you want to stay?"

"As if what we have seen is not bad enough, any storm of any size that makes landfall along this part of the coast, and especially if it comes in close to the mouth of the Ganges, will cause a catastrophe the world has not seen since Hiroshima. I must be here to report it. No one should be able to turn away from what is happening, and will happen again...in many other places."

Jennifer had finished packing and there was still forty-five minutes before they were due to leave for the airport. She set her tiny travel alarm in case she fell asleep, then flopped back on the bed, exhausted. Her thoughts turned to Li.

They had talked on a number of occasions during the trip, and she found him a fascinating conversationalist and highly dedicated and intriguing man. Very attractive. Much taller than most oriental men, his shock of black hair and smooth, handsome features gave him a commanding presence. The thought of spending time, or becoming involved, with someone with so much passion, pulled strongly at Jennifer. It's wasn't so much the sexual passion, although she was sure that would be there, and quite a change for her...but the passion for ideas, for things...for life. Li spoke with such authority. Fire seemed to always dance in his eyes. Perhaps it was her frame of mind, with the world seemingly caving in around her...but what a refuge, a haven, to be able to bury yourself emotionally, and physically in someone. If only for a while.

Her thoughts raced through those first relationships in high school when she was too serious a student and too prudish to learn much...then to college and how her liberation, the parties, that whole ridiculous, crazy scene, and then Jeffrey, had led to their relationship. *God, it must have seemed like we had so much in common, but what...or what that mattered, or would last. It's incredible how ignorant we were...naive, immature, innocent... totally oblivious to what an enduring relationship is all about.*

And poor Jeffrey. Or maybe...lucky Jeffrey. Who really knows? A good man, but not a passionate cell in his body...about anything. Well, maybe his work, but still a kind of detached passion...passionless passion. And mine burns like a fuse. And for so many things.

2012

JERUSALEM

In the first, dull, barely perceptible light of day, tear gas canisters exploded simultaneously along the one hundred and fifty meters that included the two gates on the southern wall. Following within seconds was a withering sheet of automatic weapons fire and grenades.

Kabril ran toward the triple gate, leading thirty men in gas masks into the white smoke, their weapons blazing. Two Israeli soldiers stumbled from the cloud to his right and he lifted them both off their feet and threw them backward with a swift motion and burst from the Uzi. They reached the gate and twenty of them formed a protective perimeter while the others attached the wide rope ladders to get them inside. Fire was coming back now as troops rushed from other posts, but they were pinned down, and the first group was quickly up and over. Another volley of tear gas was laid down, and the last of the men providing cover ran and scrambled across.

Kabril was now in a crouch, running low past the al Aqsa Mosque. He glanced to his right and saw Hassef's men coming from the area of the Single Gate. He wondered about Josiah and the Golden Gate, knew there had been some casualties as the last of the fighters came across...but also knew they were in the plaza. It was going well.

He dove to the ground as they received fire within fifty meters of the police post on the western wall, then motioned with a sweep of his arm. The men fanned out and directed their attack at the post where the Israelis were in fortified positions. Hearing a scream to his right, he crawled toward the motionless figure. The mask and jacket of the wounded fighter shredded in front of him and dirt, blood, and brain matter sprayed Kabril's goggles. He cleared them with his sleeve an instant before seeing the bright yellow flash of Abdul's rocket launcher. The bunker exploded, there was a second flash, then another instantaneous explosion. Kabril motioned the men forward, and again they moved low, continuing to fire. Dropping back to the ground within twenty meters of the post, ten grenades suddenly arced silently through the air. Kabril now noticed the fire and grenades coming into the post from the north that told him everyone was inside. They were up and moving forward again, then quickly all over the Israelis that remained alive.

He pulled his mask off and yelled, "Secure the prisoners, fortify your positions," knowing they must quickly protect themselves and what they had gained. Grabbing the handset from the back of his fatigues, he turned it on and spoke in a calm, steady voice. "Hassan, come in, Kabril. What is your status?"

"The gate is secure. We are deployed. We have three dead and two wounded, none seriously."

"Josiah, come in, Kabril...Josiah...do you read?" Kabril waited a moment and a voice came back.

"Roger, Kabril. We are secure. Two dead, four wounded. Two seriously."

"Hassef, come in, Kabril.....Hassef, do you..."

"This is Sahuk. Hassef is dead. The gate is secure. We have four dead and five wounded. One seriously."

Suddenly there was the deep thump of helicopter blades, and he turned back to see tracers and cannon fire rain down on his men as they ran for cover. The earth was being chewed up...men were falling...and then he saw the flash of the launcher. The gunship exploded, and there were shouts of joy as debris rained down onto the plaza.

Kabril glanced at his watch. It had been seventeen minutes since the assault began. All the gates were secured, they had established their main defensive position along the western wall where they had the protection of the police post, and, most importantly, the wall itself. They would wire it with enough explosives to crumble it into pebbles. *The Zionists will never take a chance on destroying their most sacred shrine.* His adrenaline still surged as he thought with lightning speed through everything that must be done, all the contingencies. And then he felt the elation surge through his body, and permitted himself a moment to let it overcome him. *We have taken al-Haram ash-Sharif...the Zionists Temple Mount...the Wailing Wall...in the heart of what will become Palestine. God, please let us hold it for fifteen hours...just fifteen hours.*

2012

JUDEAN DESERT, ISRAEL

John Champion stood in the middle of the compound with the rest of Alpha Company, awaiting the arrival of General Mark Engen of the Israeli Defense Forces. Engen was supposed to be there fifteen minutes ago, and everyone was becoming restless at parade rest in the heat. *It'll probably be the standard, thanks-so-much-for-your-help, give-em-hell-when-the-shooting-starts-speech. Maybe a few tips on fighting in the desert, drinking lots of water, keeping filters on everything mechanical from someone who has done this before, and anything else the good general could think of to keep up morale.*

Colonel Portman and General Engen moved quickly to the front of the company and Engen immediately began to speak. "This is not going to be the talk you expected, or I expected to give. I've just received word that an assault has been made on the Temple Mount in Jerusalem. For those of you who do not know...the Western Wall, or Wailing Wall, of the Temple Mount, is the Jewish people's holiest site. Two of the Arabs most sacred shrines are also in this area, and holding the Temple Mount will fire their troops to a fever pitch. This could well be the start of their offensive against us. We feel very strongly that the next ten to twelve hours of daylight might bring an attack. Please be ready. I thank you from the bottom of my heart...all Israelis thank you from the bottom of their hearts for your commitment and help. God be with you all."

John's flesh crawled, a shiver surged through every fiber of his body. *Well, it's here...now it starts.*

2012

DHAKA, BANGLADESH

Jennifer stared through the window of the plane, watching the palm trees bend and debris scurry across the runway ahead of the wind. After numerous delays in getting to the airport, they had been sitting here for over an hour, waiting for the plane to be serviced. The storm had moved rapidly towards them, the winds were approaching gale force, and her anxiety level was high. She knew that because of the higher temperatures of the sea water, due partially to the greenhouse, and the fact that the water's heat is the engine that drives tropical storms...this one would be bad. The pressure reading was already quite low. When the planes first officer called it a monster, she took it as affirmation that she knew her climatology. She didn't want to think of what was about to happen here, or the delays in the flight, or Cory, or anything. There were too many horrible possibilities, and certainties. Her mind was racing, jumping....and within seconds she was thinking of Cory again, safe at home, and Li, then the tens of thousands, maybe hundreds of thousands of children who would drown when the storm surge comes and the water rises...and the millions of children in other places who would die of starvation this year because of drought, not water, but made worse by the same global warming. A major war was on the brink of erupting...and chemical, biological, even nuclear weapons might be used. *Maybe the people in Idaho, or wherever, who live in underground bunkers and hoard canned food and water...maybe they've been right after all. Maybe Armageddon is coming, and this is the start.*

The plane began to move.

"Ladies and gentlemen, this is captain Beckwith. It looks like we're finally ready to go here. Sorry about the delays but we should be airborne in just a few minutes. Please check to see that your seatbelts are securely fastened. The climb out will be bumpy because of the weather, but we'll be turning back to the north and away from it and it should smooth out once we reach our cruising altitude."

The plane made the turn at the end of the runway without stopping, and Jennifer felt the surge of the engines as it straightened and accelerated dramatically. *Dear God, please keep me safe and everyone sa*...muffled explosions interrupted her prayer and she jerked forward against the belt. The engines screamed. Gasps and cries filled the cabin, and Jennifer put her head down, covered it with her arms, waited for an impact...an explosion...the plane to slide...for nothingness...waited...her mind sharply in focus on what she must do if she survived. They stopped and she was up instantly, starting for an exit.

The pilot was in the cabin, moving quickly down the aisle and shouting, "Do not try to leave the aircraft. Do not attempt to leave the aircraft. The plane is all right. The plane is all right. There was something on the end of the runway. It was not clear. Please be calm, everything is all right." The pilot turned and hurried back into the cockpit as the same message came through the speakers from one of the flight attendants..

"Wasn't that an explosion? Did you hear it?" Hal Hollins, a science writer, leaned across the aisle and questioned Jennifer.

"Yes, it sounded like that to me." She turned her head toward the window and closed her eyes, hoping no one else would try to talk to her. Her heart pounded.

There was no word further word from the crew as the plane remained motionless on the runway for what seemed to Jennifer like ten or fifteen minutes. Then the voice came over the intercom. "This is Captain Beckwith. The plane is all right. No damage. The rest of the news is not so good, and I don't think you folks would want me to sugar coat it. There were three explosions at the end of the runway just after we accelerated. That's why we stopped. Seems they were mortars. I'm going to read you a message exactly as it was just read to me by the tower.

"In support of our Arab brothers we demand that the United States Government remove all troops and military equipment from the soil of what is now called Israel but is rightfully Palestine. If this pullout does not start within twenty four hours we will destroy the United Airlines aircraft that is now on the runway at Dhaka. It is signed Shanti Bahani."

Their was silence inside the plane for a few moments and then she heard Hal Hollins say to no one in particular, "Damned idiots. Twenty-four hours. Don't they know within six this plane, their mortars and everybody's asses are all going to be floating toward the Himalayas."

2012

WASHINGTON, D.C.

"Damn it, Joe…hell of a serve," Sam said to his friend as they walked toward each other on the change-over. "So much for you working hard at anything other than improving your game. At our age, you don't find that kind of additional pace unless you're spending more time on the tennis court and less pounding out stories."

"Now, now, be nice," Joe laughed. "Maybe it's technology… I'm hooked on the latest in those mega caffeine energy drinks. Or it could be our eyes don't pick the ball up quite as well as they used to. Don't know about you…but nothing of mine works as well as it used to." The guitar break from *Stairway to Heaven* played inside Joe's tennis bag and he moved to retrieve his phone. "Sorry, Sam, let me see who it is."

After answering, Joe was silent, listening intently, not moving, with the cell phone to his ear. "Jesus, Adam. Jesus Christ. I'm on my way." Joe's arm dropped to his side, his hand holding the phone limply. His face was ashen, his eyes as alarmed as Sam had ever seen them.

"Jesus. A container ship just blew sky high in Savannah. Big explosion, killed ten to twenty people on board and alongside the dock. There's a preliminary report of heavy radioactive readings. Dirty bomb is a good bet," Joe said, his voice conveying defeat.

"Timing," Sam said. "The Temple Mount, now this. If confirmed, it's devastating news on its own. But I've got a very bad feeling."

2012

JUDEAN DESERT, ISRAEL

As darkness fell across the desert, John wondered if he could relax even a bit. They had been waiting for the attack for ten hours, in full anti-chemical battle gear except for the mask...weapons ready, artillery manned, tanks deployed. The prolonged tension and fear made his whole body ache, and along with the heat, had reduced him to physical exhaustion.

His mind had begun to numb from the continuous cavalcade of thoughts and ruminations it generated. He had gone over and over everything he must do, when it started, to keep his men and himself alive and fighting. What it's like to be hit...to die...to watch someone die...to kill...his parents...Shawn...George Burnett...the effects of nerve gas or an anthrax bomb...seeing the nuclear flash from Tel Aviv? These thoughts and a thousand others had passed through his consciousness. *Maybe the attack won't come today...the Temple Mount could be unrelated...there are so many groups. With darkness we'll have the advantage again. God, I'd like to get out of this stuff. Shouldn't have any trouble sleeping tonight...if I'm still here. Crazy, I haven't been sleeping, and now on the scariest day of my life I think I can.* Lifting the plastic bottle to his lips, he finished off his second or third gallon of water of the day. For the first time, John felt the urge to urinate. His sweat poured nonstop.

The order came to get some sleep and he headed to the latrine. A few minutes later he was out of the protective suit, stripped to his underwear, and on the bunk in the camouflaged tent. *How can I possibly enjoy laying here as much as I am, how can I possibly feel this good when I should be terrified...when I may be about to die? A few hours to relax before daylight. Maybe this is the ultimate extension of time...a couple of hours before certain horror, and serenity shows up. Or maybe the mind has a safety valve. After a certain amount of fear and tension, at some point, it automatically shifts.*

Gigantic, hundred-foot-long shells under pink and yellow parachutes floated slowly down towards him. The explosion instantly jolted John to a sitting position on the bunk. Trying to shake the dream from his mind, the next explosion momentarily confused him. Then his entire body stiffened.

Off the cot in an instant, he grappled with the suit and boots, then shot out of the tent and ran, his rifle in one hand and mask in the other. Two more rounds exploded just outside the compound, and he could hear yells and commands. Reaching his men, John checked to be sure everyone was where they should be, had all their equipment, then looked out across the desert...at blackness. He fumbled with the night vision goggles in his pocket...finally getting them on. The concertina wire glowed an eerie green, but he saw nothing else. Huddled against the sandbags, he waited. They all waited. Their own artillery began to answer, then two more incoming rounds exploded outside. Smoke wafted over them. The scream of jets added to the rising, wild, and discordant assault of sounds. John felt fear, but it wasn't gut-wrenching.

For a long time he crouched, not moving, mesmerized, calm, watching and listening to the amazing spectacle unfolding above him - the glow of afterburners and laser-thin red tracers crisscrossing the pitch black sky as fighter jets engaged each other and anti-air defenses in their deadly, radar eyes-only sorties and dogfights. Occasional bright flashes told him when a plane had been destroyed, but not whose soldier died. He knew terror and violent death was happening in the sky, but from the ground the whole scene seemed surreal, strangely disconnected. After the initial volley of near-miss artillery rounds, they had not taken any more fire. His watch read one a.m. It had been an hour and a half since it started.

There was a sudden, shattering explosion, then smoke and shouts filled the air. John instinctively ducked his head as the concussion from the second round slammed into him, and he felt a burning sensation in his leg as yet another hit erupted along the wall.

"Down! Down! Masks! Get your masks on," he screamed. There was a string of explosions just outside and the sudden blast from ground-hugging jets on the bombing run. Glancing down his row of men, he saw no one who looked injured. As he turned toward the center of the compound, he watched the haze of smoke clear enough to reveal the sickening sight of crumpled bodies, and one man sitting with his arm and shoulder missing. There were screams and a cry of "medic" coming from the thick smoke on the far end of the sandbagged wall.

John felt the fear crush down on him, much harder than he had ever known. Fighting the urge to freeze, he forced himself up and looked into the night. Still nothing. A sense of focus replaced the fear, and he realized he would be able to do whatever he needed to do. Another round slammed into the ground behind him, then another. The smoke was so thick, so enveloping, that he couldn't see anything. More planes streaked overhead, and more rounds and bombs exploded just in back of him. He waited to be hit...or for nothingness. The chaotic confusion of noise, dust, smoke and cries smothered him. He thought to glance at his sleeve and raised his arm to his eyes. The red dots were glowing.

"Chemicals! Chemicals!" he shouted. Moving in a crouch down the row of men, he checked to be sure all their masks were on and they had injected themselves. When he was sure they had all followed his orders, he removed the plastic container from the zippered compartment on his pant leg, took off the cap, and slammed the six inch long needle through all the layers of clothing and into his shoulder.

The longest night of his life wore on, with more planes, bombs, rockets, artillery, and the constant rumbling of distant tank battles.

There were two more hits on their position, and more maimed and dead. With only small spotlights to illuminate the injured and assess the damage through the haze of smoke, sand and dust, the noise, the cries and smell of powder...it all seemed to John truly a scene from some surreal, dreamlike hell.

So this is war. It's not about land or beliefs or politicians or generals. It's about good, innocent kids being blown apart in a goddamned desert or thousands of feet up in the sky. Kids with parents, brothers and sisters, wives, husbands and children who love them, and will be lost without them. Kids who die, or are maimed or mentally scarred for the rest of their lives, and in most cases don't have a clue to the real reasons the presidents and kings of greed, power and ego sent them into the inferno. It's insane. Are we more civilized now than in the days armies dropped burning oil on their enemies? Hell no, just more progressive. Each year we learn how to kill more people faster. And that's it. The whole thing. The determining factor in how the greatest civilizations in history do business is still which sides' poor innocent sons-of-bitches slaughter more of the other sides' poor innocent sons-of-bitches.' It's sensitivity training, self-actualization and animal rights at home...and barbaric, mass slaughter of human beings abroad.

John noticed helicopters ahead of them firing tracers with a steep trajectory. The tanks and artillery sounded closer. An hour ago he was told they were within ten miles. Looking ahead into the blackness, he could see flashes from more muzzles now, and they were brighter.

"All right, men, we should be getting some fire from the tanks soon. Is everybody ready?"

"Are you scared, sergeant?" Cristol, next to him, spoke in a barely audible voice.

"Hell yes, have been all night."

"Remember those guys that fought in Nam telling us that if you live long enough you kind of learn to like it? When you get good at it you can get hooked on the rush."

"Yeah, I remember," John replied.

"There aren't enough days or battles left in the couple of million years before the sun explodes for that to happen to me. How about you?"

"Yeah...I agree. I goddamn sure as hell agree."

John stared through the opening in the sandbags. He knew how much it would change if they had some light. It was a matter of what got there first.

A flight of fighters thundered by just overhead, and bombs and rockets exploded beneath them. More helicopters darted into the battle, and he knew they were throwing everything they had to keep them off the camp. Through the goggles he was able to barely make out their own tanks ahead. *A little light, must be a little light. Even with night vision...there's just so damned many of them. God, give us little light...and please keep me...all these good men safe Lord.* The noise was deafening...tanks, artillery, planes, bombs...and all at close range.

The sandbag wall to his left suddenly exploded and three of his men were thrown twenty feet back and into the air. John quickly crawled toward them, stared for a moment at the mangled bodies, then moved back toward the gaping hole in the wall. Another direct hit sent bodies flying farther down. He looked through the new breach in the wall. The staccato of automatic weapons signaled the incoming fire was close, but he still saw nothing through the smoke, falling sand, and faint light. His men started firing blindly. Screams and cries added to the hellacious noise and chaos. The wall exploded again just to his right and something slammed into his shoulder and knocked him backward. Struggling up he reached for the man laying across his legs and turned him over. "Private Cristol" was on the name tag and half of his neck and head were missing. John wretched violently, almost vomited.

God, please help me.

Rolling over to stay low, he moved back behind the cover of the sandbags and crawled from man to man. "All right, stay calm...take your time and aim...they'll never get through the mines." Putting his rifle through an opening he began firing...into the smoke, in an arc. He could see nothing.

Saleh was moving quickly now, screaming louder and louder as the fear rose and gripped him like a giant, clawed hand. "Allah Akbar! Allah Akbar! Death to the Zionists!"

A mine exploded and the boy running beside him was blown into the air. Another went off in front of Saleh and a large piece of a body slammed into him, knocking him down. Up quickly and running again...he screamed even louder. "Allah Akbar! Allah Akbar!"

2012

NEPAL

Sliding quickly down the wild, boiling river, the large raft moved faster, the rapids were more frequent. I was in the very back, with a tight grip on the handholds. With the excitement and adrenaline rush, with all eyes glued on the approaching white water, no one would notice when I fell out. When I didn't come back up they would assume I had drowned, and only then discover the lack of information on the man with only one name.

I had finally received instructions from the Council on how to find The Wise One, and I was anxious. The situation for the humans and the planet was not good, by far the worst since my initial visit years ago, and continued to deteriorate rapidly. I had assumed a human form as instructed. While in this I form I would have all the feelings and emotions of the humans, and be susceptible to their injuries and death.

"Luggalor, are you all right, lad?" One of the guides looked back and yelled above the roar of the river.

"Yes, I am all right."

"Are you enjoying yourself?"

"Yes, I am enjoying myself. It is wonderful...exhilarating." And it truly was...the motion, the noise, the rushing water...the cool, brisk air against my human skin, the beauty along the banks, the hawk circling overhead. I wished for a moment I could have made the entire trip.

I asked the guide to tell me when we approached the rapids known as 'Maelstrom'. It was there I must go into the water, locate and enter the hydraulic, then find the opening and be pulled through it. The guides explained the dangers of this particular hydraulic before they put the raft into the river, emphasizing its violence and the deaths it had caused. A sort of whirlpool, it could suck a person below the surface, and once trapped, the forces of the water were too strong to overcome and the unlucky human would drown. It was located just below the biggest drop at the 'Maelstrom' rapids.

I had assumed the form of a small male human so it would be easier to fit through the opening, and I would have less of a chance of being injured. My first choice was to take the form of one of the precious human children, but a child would not have been allowed on the raft alone. I hoped I was small enough.

The raft suddenly accelerated dramatically, began to undulate, slide across and bounce off rocks. A loud rushing noise came from forward of the raft, and I tightened my grip.

The guide turned and shouted, "Maelstrom dead ahead, hold on tight lad."

The raft dipped, then surged forward, as if airborne...again and again. The roar was thunderous...and then, suddenly, we were free of the water as we dropped, nose down, toward a gigantic, bubbling caldron of white foam.

I squeezed the hand holds even tighter, then realized...*this is it*. Letting go, I leaned back and suddenly had nothing below me but air. My back slammed into the water...the cold shock sucked the breath from my human lungs. Knowing I must get under immediately or I would pass the opening, I turned and thrust my head and shoulders down. There was an immediate tug, my body was violently buffeted, and I began tumbling and spinning. I could not stop, or tell up from down...the power of the water was enormous. I tried to reach my hand out to feel for the opening, but could barely move it from my body against the pressure. My human lungs began to ache. With all the strength I could muster I thrust my outstretched hand forward and the tips of my fingers felt something hard…smooth…a rock. Groping, I felt an indentation. My fingers were pulled away by the force of the rushing water. My breath all but gone, I jammed them back against the rock and found a space. Straining, I began to pull myself forward, then suddenly I was sucked with tremendous speed into a passage so narrow I could feel every inch of my body squeezing between the smooth, hard sides. My sight mechanisms closed tightly as my body accelerated. I knew I must take a breath, even though in my human form I realized I would die. As I opened my mouth I sensed I was suddenly flying through the air, then I landed head first in something soft. Lying motionless, I gasped for air. Finally convinced I had breathed enough to keep from dying, sure I was still alive, I sat up and opened my sight mechanisms.

There was only the faintest hint of light, coming from the distance. As my sight mechanisms adjusted to the darkness, I saw that I was sitting on a narrow, four-foot wide path of soft, loose dirt. On my right was a wall that to my touch felt like damp rock, and on my left a dark chasm that appeared to have no bottom. Standing up, my head hit the wall that I now knew curved out above me and over the path. In a crouch, I began to move toward the light, with my right hand sliding along the wall to make sure I was as far away from the edge and black gorge as I could get. A strange sensation…the humans sense of fear. Could be debilitating if left unchecked.

The path angled sharply down, and I was slow and methodical with my steps. After perhaps a hundred feet and a bend to the left, I could see it continued down and straight again for some distance. The glow was still ahead for me to follow. Whether the light was stronger or my sight mechanisms were adjusting, I could now make out the gray, pockmarked rock wall that I caressed as I moved.

Coming to another turn in the path, I inched around it and was startled by what was directly ahead.. Huge, craggy, cone-like formations, gray and ominous, hung from the blackness above. I noticed that the walls curve was no longer so low that I must crouch, and I straightened up and stopped for a moment to look around. Moving again, I continued to hug the wall. The chasm was still there...still appeared to have no bottom.

There were two more turns in rapid succession. The light had increased and the hanging formations now sparkled as if each contained millions of tiny pieces of crystal. The path turned again. Similar formations now rose out of the chasm, their ends jutting just past the ends of those descending from above...forming a jagged, sparkling, overlapping formation that reminded me of a set of enormous teeth I had seen on the large carnivores of planet 1003's jungles and seas. The path continued to wind downward, although not as steeply as before. The glow of light remained ahead, noticeably brighter now.

The formations began to take on a gold, shimmering cast, and I started to walk faster and more deliberately, although still favoring the wall, with my sight mechanisms darting up and down, side to side, so I would miss nothing. The wall now sparkled with gold hued crystals that were embedded in layers of reddish, orange rock.

My fingers suddenly felt heat coming from the wall as they slid along it. A sinister looking steam began to rise from the chasm, and my human face started to drip salt filled water that stung my sight mechanisms. The path steepened again, and I slowed my pace. The heat quickly became overwhelming, and I heard what sounded like liquid bubbling from the depths of the black abyss only inches away. The steam became a thick cloud, and the formations all but disappeared into it. I could barely see anything and I stopped, terrified that the path might end in the fog and I would fall into the boiling pit. Human fear is no doubt debilitating. Panic gripped me, and I started to turn and run back to the entrance. Then I remembered the entrance, and The Wise One, and I stood very still, and tried to calm myself. Once more I started down the path, but took only small, shuffling steps, my hand on the hot rock wall as long as I could stand it, then reaching for it again as soon as the pain from the heat subsided. I was creeping along ever so slowly, the steam continuing to thicken...when suddenly, without warning, I was falling, dropping straight down. I closed my sight mechanisms, heard my own scream...as I continued to fall...toward the boiling liquid. I splashed in and submerged, but rather than pain a luxuriant warmth enveloped me and coursed through every fiber of my human form. Hanging for a moment, suspended, in this womblike place, the need to breath reminded me that I had to.

Rising through the luxurious liquid, I broke the surface to look out over a shimmering gold lake inside a spectacular, cathedral-like cave. The walls appeared to be solid crystal. Shafts of soft, white light poured down and fanned out from above, reflecting off the water and sparkling walls to create a magnificent, glowing, golden haze. Flowers were everywhere...encircling the lake, along the walls. Yellow, pink and red roses... white lilies...orchids of purple, blue and gold, and many varieties I did not know from my time on 1003. All lovely. I had never seen, nor imagined, such a magnificent place. On this planet or any other.

The water held me easily on the surface with a soothing buoyancy, and I was in no hurry to leave it. I stayed very still, let it relax my bruised body and quiet my racing mind. Tilting my head back, I closed my sight mechanisms, sucked in a long breath, then exhaled.

"Luggalor." The voice was gentle, but strong, and flowed like warm honey.

Standing at the end of the lake was a beautiful, statuesque female human clad in a long, flowing white gown. Cascading light from above illuminated her in a lovely haze, played off her waist-length flaxen hair, and it shimmered with a brilliant radiance. "You must be hungry, thirsty, and tired. Now that you are in a human form you must nourish and replenish yourself." She gestured to the side with her arm and open palm. "There is food and drink and also something to dry yourself with, and fresh clothes. There is a bed for you to sleep on. I will return when you have awakened and we will talk. I am glad you have come."

"I would..." I started to speak as she turned and disappeared into the center of the rays of light.

Climbing from the lake, I walked to a low, marble table surrounded by thick cushions. Beside the table was a bed, also of marble, with intricately carved head and foot boards that resembled the front and rear of a sleigh. On the bed was fine silk bedding and pillows, all pale green, and a male human's white linen shirt and trousers rested across the foot board. A pair of soft slippers were just below on the floor.

I stripped the soaked clothes off and dried myself, then put on the clean set and sat on the cushions beside the table. Silver bowls overflowed with fruit, berries, nuts and vegetables. There was hot bread with a thick, wonderful aroma, and deep red wine in a crystal decanter. A slice of lemon floated in a silver pitcher of cool, fresh water.

Eating and drinking heartily, I thought what a pleasant experience nourishing one's body could be for a human if they have adequate access to food and drink. But it must also be quite a bother, having to do it numerous times each day. I became aware of a sound, somewhat familiar, and very faint. It gradually became louder, and I smiled as I recognized the lovely strains of the Bach Fugue.

The food and wine were so delightful, and their presentation, the setting, and the music so exquisite...that I ate and drank considerably more than was needed for nourishment. My eyelids felt heavy when I finally finished, and it was all I could do to make my way the few feet to the bed and tumble in before falling asleep. Those last moments before the unconscious, sleep-state the humans need was, at least in this case, delightfully comfortable.

Coming awake, I again stared in amazement. The chamber seemed more beautiful than when I had first seen it, if that was possible. The marble table had been moved to the center of a small island in the lake where the rays of light rained down in concentration and brilliantly, but softly, illuminated a single, silver vase filled with beautiful flowers, and a matching pitcher and goblet. Two large, high-backed chairs, covered in what appeared to be white satin, were to the side of the table, facing each other.

I climbed off the bed, slid my feet into the slippers, and began to move toward the narrow marble bridge with gold hand rails that led to the island, when suddenly I realized the female human in the white gown was standing between the chairs. Startled by her sudden appearance, beauty and magnificent presence at this close distance...I stopped dead in my tracks.

"Come, Luggalor, please sit down. We have much to discuss and we should be comfortable."

I took small, slow steps...mesmerized by all that surrounded me...but also a bit unsure. My mind churned, but without any thoughts I could hold. I glanced around, then at her, then around again, until I reached the island, and then the chair. I sat down.

We were separated by about six feet and the center shafts of soft white light, which bathed and slightly obscured her with the lovely, bright haze. Her face looked old and wise and young at the same time, without the wrinkles and sagging skin that I had come to associate with humans as they age. Her thick, golden hair was pulled back from around her face. Her simple elegance and beauty were magnificent.

"You were very wise to discover the lens and duplicate them. I would like to know your thoughts on how they affect the humans, and impact the critical issues on this planet that you have seen. Her voice was so calming, so soothing, that I felt my apprehension and anxiety melt into a warm glow. Subtle excitement, mixed with a feeling of comfort and ease.

"You are the Wise One? The human I was told I must find?"

"The answer to your first question is yes. The answer to your second is more complicated. And not important at this time. Please begin with your story."

"There are so many diverse and often harmful thoughts and actions by so many humans on matters of great importance," I said. "There seems to be little universal sense of what is right or wrong, or what is accepted as truth, or at least no consistent agreement on what it is. And it all seems to start with the lens."

"Luggalor, when a child is born their lens is clear. There are no distorting filters that cause distorted perceptions of information processed through their senses. An infant will awaken in the morning and greet everything and everyone with a smile...with enthusiasm for experiencing...for adventure and learning. And that child will feel...will give and accept...that most powerful and positive human dynamic...the dynamic that melds thought with feeling, and comes from the depths of the soul. Love. Their perceptions are clear and true. This is the natural state. A state based on a Truth that fosters universal harmony and is lodged in every thread of matter, every action, from the past, through the present, and into the future...on this planet and throughout the great breadth of all creation. It comes from the Gods, the Spirits, the Prophets...who are one...and who will forever be guardians of the enlightenment and salvation that comes from striving to understand and live according to the Truth...from living a life filled with love."

She continued. "As there are no distortions of the lens at birth, the Truth resides in the heart of every human, waiting to be discovered, nurtured and followed. New little humans have to learn how not to trust, how to judge falsely, and how to hate. With the explosion in access to unrestricted communication and information that can destroy fact and civility through appeals to insecurity and fear - evil lessons are more available than ever to the adults whom the young learn from and emulate. Make no mistake about it, Luggalor...the fresh, fertile minds of the earth's children can be easily manipulated into following the many paths that lead away from the Truth. Paths that lead toward the ignorance, greed, and self absorption that serve the ego and its world of illusions...that obscure and eventually obliterate the Truth and eliminate any chance at true peace and harmony through love."

"When a child's eyes first open...this is when the process begins that will determine if they will be wise and productive and content...enlightened...if they will understand the Truth and contribute to the welfare of the planet and its inhabitants...or if they will be ignorant and dominated by self absorption, greed and the illusionary world the ego creates to survive. The incredible amount of information a human absorbs in a lifetime, and particularly in their early years, can form filters on their lens with alarming efficiency. If these filters obscure the Truth and provide defenses against threats to an exalted temple of ego, they must be eliminated. But it is much harder to remove them and clear the lens, to teach a person with distorted perceptions to embrace the natural state of the Truth, than it is to nurture and develop it from the beginning."

"Everything on this planet, in the universe, is connected." Her voice softened slightly. "And everything, regardless of how seemingly insignificant, must work in symphony to achieve the natural balance and harmony that has been inherent in the grand design since creation. But humans, because of the great power of their minds, have a much more telling effect on the prosperity or destruction of the planet and its life than any other form of life. By far the most critical factor in how humans handle this enormous responsibility is what they learn, the filters that form on their lens from what they learn, and how the filters affect their perceptions, thoughts and actions. There are only distorted perceptions of reality and the Truth. A peaceful, harmonious world can only be maintained if the lenses are clear, if the Truth thrives in the minds, hearts, and souls of the humans."

"Individual humans think so differently, and there are so many critically important issues in so many different places on the planet...is their nothing out of their control, nothing that is not related to the lens and distortion of the filters?" I asked.

"There will always be sadness and tragedy in the world, even evil, at least as measured through human emotion and empathy. Natural disasters, mental and physical problems or deficiencies from birth, disease or accidents, even tragedies due to evil in a relatively few resistant human minds...will never be totally eliminated. It is in the grand design of the Gods...that there will always be challenges and problems to confront. But the critical and potentially lethal problems now facing the planet and its life can be dealt with in ways that will greatly improve the lives of millions and put the planet on a road to harmony and prosperity rather than ruin. The Gods assured solutions when they created the extraordinary power and potential of the human mind. The challenge is for enough humans to live by the principals of the Truth so critical issues such as environmental destruction, poverty, starvation, disease and infant mortality, the threat of weapons of mass destruction, war and terrorism...can be dealt with effectively."

"Luggalor, with relatively few exceptions, every child, every adult, has the potential to learn and accept the Truth, to incorporate into their life a deep sense of spirituality, self-worth, morality and responsibility, and acquire the knowledge and skills to become a content, productive member of this remarkable species...and contribute in a meaningful way to peace and harmony for this remarkable world. There are significant differences among humans in their mental and physical capabilities to perform tasks. But there is an enormous variety and number of tasks that serve a useful purpose. If the Truth guides the life of enough humans, future generations will have far fewer negative influences and distorted lens, and a much greater opportunity to live a life of peace and harmony. The potential is there for every human to contribute and enjoy life to a meaningful fullness, and for the daunting problems you have witnessed to be overcome."

"What exactly is this truth you keep referring to?" I asked.

"Understanding the Truth is simple. You must only understand Love. For love is the Truth. Love and all of its manifestations. Love and all of its gifts and responsibilities."

"Love is filled with an open mind. And forgiveness. Not only of others, but yourself. And empathy. And making the focus of your life giving rather than taking. The Gods designed a world that can exist in perfect balance...a world in which all things are connected and interrelate with all others. Feeling and showing love for the rest of the world...always... is the key. But to do that each human must first love themselves."

She continued. "Each individual has the same inherent worth and value. Each is as cherished by the Gods and all of creation as any other. Regardless of mental, or physical capabilities, or status within a society. Making one's own life better is perfectly acceptable...is in fact a key ingredient in achieving natural harmony. As is enjoying life to the fullest. If one then feels and shows the same love for others as they do for themselves, they can become as successful by their own measure as possible, yet they will never act in ways that harm others. They will only do what is right for the planet and its life."

"There are no imperfections, Luggalor. Only imperfect perceptions. Caused by distorted filters on the lens. False judgment, and the prejudice and hate it inspires, are among the Truth's worst enemies. No loving thought can be unfairly judgmental. Those thoughts only come from the ego and its world of defense and illusion. Blaming others is often a way to deflect personal guilt. Love is about healing, about responding to cries of pain and pleas for help. Love is about releasing fear, about turning darkness into light. It is about teaching empathy, forgiveness and acceptance...about teaching the power of the Truth. Love is everything a human should be, and everything they come from.

They only have to accept their true destiny...a life dedicated to letting love for themselves, their families, all life and the planet, guide their actions and thoughts. A life filled with an unbreakable bond of caring. And the more an individual's thoughts and actions reflect love and concern for the welfare of others, the easier success and contentment in their own life will be to attain."

"I used the lens of so many humans who do not live by the principals you say are so critically important...by love and the Truth. Teaching them...changing their perspectives...it would seem to be an incredibly difficult task. How can each of the humans learn these lessons...and keep their lens from becoming distorted by filters that produce harmful thoughts and actions? And if they are distorted, how can they be cleared?"

"It will take faith and diligent effort by each human...and time. The grand design of the Gods is that each person spend their lives becoming the best possible person they can be. This is the means, not the end. The end is the collective effect of all the 'best possible people'...striving to make the 'best possible world', resulting in the planet attaining its potential of evolving into a place of harmony and peace. This transformation to the Truth is inextricably tied to inner peace within each individual, as the planet's discord and strife is in reality the discord and strife of many humans projected outward. It is really about education, Luggalor. Learning the Truth, accepting the healing and changes that must take place to embrace it, and then teaching it to others."

She paused for a moment, her eyes directly on mine. I felt the warmth, the passion...the wisdom of her message as I began to speak. "Will you tell me exactly how the humans can be taught to make the changes you speak of? And will you tell me how I can help them if I stay on the planet?"

"The first part of your request I will grant...the second part we will discuss in time. All the problems you have encountered on your visits to earth can be traced to some form of ignorance or greed, and their inevitable consequence, an obsession with self-interest over the greater good. Ignorance in the large sense meaning ignorance of the Truth... reflected in the day-to-day thoughts and actions that are in conflict with the principals of the Truth. Greed and obsessive self-interest serve the ego in many ways, from a compulsion to accumulate excessive wealth or power, to the fierce defensiveness that often protects a destructive sense of pride. Ignorance births greed, and a dedication to greed perpetuates ignorance."

Her voice was calm, measured, but laced with concern. "Ignorance and greed show their ugly faces millions of times each day, in thoughts and acts that adversely affect the tiniest of creatures and the largest of nations. They cause a supposedly well-educated leader in the field of commerce to ignore the tremendous harm he does by abusing the environment, or neglecting the financial interests of client companies, because he is a slave to questionable measures that will squeeze a few more percentage points of profit from his market. They cause ruling elites to ignore the cumulative damage done to their societies and people by their policies...because the establishment and preservation of their power and privileges is their primary guiding principle. Elected and appointed officials in the most democratic of nations do irreparable harm through an obsession with preserving their positions at the cost of policies that are clearly more in step with the common good. There is a school of thought which many humans subscribe to - that a certain amount of greed is good, even desirable, that it fosters motivation and healthy competition. This is true on a limited level. The problem arises when an individual's level of greed is stronger than their commitment to the welfare of others and the planet."

"Yes, I understand what you are saying. But I want to hear more about solutions."

"There is one resource, Luggalor, that is a critical part of the solution to the planet's daunting problems. You will remember I said that each individual must focus as much on giving as taking.

Giving can take the form of money, resources, or time. Volunteerism. Whether it is individuals acting as mentors for children in ghettos, willingly paying taxes for better educational systems and health care for all, donating larger percentages of excess wealth, organizations providing financial and human resources for charitable causes, corporations funding research into cures for disease and clean energy sources, or a government contributing aid to underdeveloped countries – a high level of giving is necessary. Fortunately, the human and natural resources are available. Again, the challenge is properly educating and channeling the minds of enough humans to ensure wise choices are made for utilizing the planet's enormous human and material wealth. Wealth that can, without a doubt, solve the most intractable of problems."

"The education that will keep distorting filters off the lens must start from the day of birth, and never stop during a lifetime. For children, the best teachers are parents."

"But many children don't have parents, or parents who seem to understand and live by the truth," I said. "Who will teach them from the beginning?"

"Parents must teach. It is the most important and sacred task humans have. That means parents must be educated and enlightened as to their enormous responsibility, how to teach and what must be taught – the great lessons of morality and ethics, a responsibility to give, compassion and empathy, as well as the pursuit of the specialized skills that will enable their children to be productive. They must also realize that the most effective way they teach, whether intended or not, whether the lessons are good or bad, is by their example. Children must have positive role models...role models they can emulate."

"But you are right, Luggalor. In many cases parents are not there, or are not, or will not, become effective teachers. There must be alternatives for their children from an early age. Facilities where they can spend their days and nights, if necessary, and be cared for, nurtured, and loved. Where they can learn the basic social skills and principles of respect, sharing and giving, the concept of universal dignity, and the rewards of accomplishment. Enlightened individuals, those dedicated to the Truth, must give the time necessary to pass their knowledge along to the next generations, as well as to others who can join them in teaching these next generations. Local, regional and national charitable organizations, churches, parents groups, the private sector, governments...must all assume an intense dedication to reaching and affecting as many children as possible, as early as possible. Professional teachers must be extremely dedicated and motivated. Their training and pay must be exemplary. Teaching is the most important job on the planet, and the status and compensation for true professionals must be elevated to reflect this."

"You talk about cost in terms of great sums of money, and there being the resources to pay for it. But many of the thoughts and actions I have observed reflect a reluctance to pay for anything other than what each human thinks will benefit them, their family, or their enterprises in the near future,"

"Ignorance and greed, Luggalor. Whether it is through peers, teachers, leaders, churches, or the media...people must be made aware of the magnitude of the problems...and the necessity of paying the cost to solve them. They must realize that refusing to accept their share of the burden will surely cause them to bear their share of the consequences. In an ever-shrinking world the problems of one group of people in one location often has an adverse affect on many other groups of people in distant places. Local problems quickly become national, then global problems. Again, the irony – when humans dedicate their lives to contributing to the welfare of others and the planet, they inevitably live lives filled with a sense of peace and fulfillment. Greed and self-absorption are truly false gods. "

"But where will the money actually come from, how will it be generated, who will decide to spend it, and on what?" I asked.

"If enough humans live by the Truth, adequate financial resources will be a natural by-product of this transformation. What is needed is each person's dedication to contributing to the common good and solutions to the immediate, critical problems that are causing so much suffering and harm and threaten so much more Private sector companies and organizations, churches, or individuals can contribute money in a number of ways, as can governments through grants, tax relief, or outright funding".

"Throughout the world there has been a recent, dramatic shift toward market economies, and to a lesser extent, democratic, or at least representative, governments. Some form of legitimate voice of the people in their government, coupled with the opportunity to participate in a system of private enterprise that will have a direct impact on improving the quality of their lives, is certainly the most equitable and ethical of systems, and will encourage widespread participation and productivity. But if a government and economic system based on something closer to socialism or a central authority is administered with true concern and compassion for the people...if the work of individuals involved in such a system reflect a commitment to the principals of the Truth...the type of system doesn't matter. What matters is that all societies' citizens follow their hearts...and their hearts are filled with compassion and giving. The problem is not necessarily the system, but rather the ignorance and greed of the ruling elite or governing body. Again, irony. An obsession with maintaining their positions, power and privileges - at the expense of the positive evolution of the state and the welfare of its citizens - has and always will be the main cause of the downfall of oppressive governments, as it has always been one of the primary reasons for creating them."

She continued. "Again, destructive dynamics are easy to see in the most democratic of governments and free market economies. Elected officials make the task of keeping their jobs their paramount concern and stop at nothing to please those relatively few powerful and wealthy individuals and organizations that can assure their longevity...and, in some cases, their personal gain.

Constituencies that can deliver critical votes are courted by spreading lies and fear. Leaders of industry and commerce display their greed through an obsession with exorbitant profits and personal rewards...the common good be damned. A sort of holy crusade for self-interest...to the detriment of the system, the people, and more and more...the planet."

"It will take great sacrifice to secure the human effort to solve the critical problems you have seen. The rulers, leaders and officials, whatever the system, must make the right choices, and many of those choices will be hard. They must develop and use their conscience, rather than their greed. And the people...they must open their minds to the true facts, learn the issues, hold their government responsible if the right choices are not made, and accept the responsibility of helping to pay the cost. A critical mass of humans must become givers as well as takers. A critical mass of humans must become accountable."

"Accountability for actions and performance is absolutely necessary, Luggalor. For individuals, and organizations, and governments. For children and students, for teachers, politicians and captains of industry. The evolution of the human mind...the ability to choose freely...mandates the responsibility of accountability."

I sat silent for a time, let her words sink in, then asked, "How much time will it take...for the changes to take place? Is there enough time?

"There is time. But no time to waste. Education. Whether learned from enlightened parents, or teachers, or through the teachings of Buddha, or Mohammed, or Christ. All the major religions are based on the principals of the Truth."

"Developed nations with vibrant economies must make substantive changes quickly to lead the way. They are capable of leading and their citizens must insist they accept the challenge. Standards in critical areas such as education, human rights, health care, arms control and environmental protection must be universally sustained."

"With proper motivation and resources, a person's knowledge can evolve quickly…in only months or a few years…to the point there will be significant changes to their thoughts and actions. Many epiphanies occur, and many more can. But only if effective motivation, an understanding of the power of knowledge, and quality education are available to all."

"Since I have been coming to 1003, there has been a rapid evolution in digital communications, and in particular the internet," I said. There is so much misinformation, so much harmful coercion, and so many humans have access to it. Isn't this teaching humans to stray farther from the Truth? Isn't it creating, or hardening the distorting filters?"

"As each individual must be diligent in opening their mind to discovering and learning the principals of the Truth, they must reject concepts, thoughts and actions that are enemies of the truth. Many only search for information to reinforce their current beliefs. For those who are not enlightened, who do not have an open mind and have distorting filters on their lens - emotional appeals, particularly those that play on their fears, have an extremely strong appeal. Much harm is done in the world by those consumed with greed and power who utilize this dynamic of control that is so harmful to the common good. There are relatively few individuals that do not now have access to the worldwide web, and there is much information available there that teaches hate, prejudice, and other arch enemies of the Truth. Each human must learn to ignore those who teach what is destructive and embrace and learn from those who teach the path to enlightenment. They must eliminate the distorting filters on their lens rather than allow more to form. And those who knowingly spread falsehoods and misleading information to benefit their own personal agendas, and in particular those in positions of power who do…the Gods are always unhappy with them."

"There is a war going on now. It is horrible and senseless. Could the educational systems and opportunities you have outlined have prevented this tragedy?"

"Of all the mistakes humans have made...war is the worst. It must be perceived in all its true horror rather than romanticized. If people understand the Truth and the possibilities of a harmonious world, they will refuse to sanction or condone it, leaders will be reluctant to enter into it if they have no support...and armies will refuse to fight if they no longer believe in the cause. The hope must be that some day enough people will see the folly of war and realize they can live together and settle their differences without slaughtering each other. Adhering to the principals of The Truth will eliminate many of the leaders dominated by ego and greed; leaders who are ultimately responsible for starting most wars...leaders who are willing to sacrifice so many innocent lives for the purpose of obtaining or maintaining addictive, ruinous power. But until the day comes when the world is led by enlightened leaders, there must be strong, effective measures to prevent the terrible scourge of armed conflict, as there must be to lessen the cataclysmic horrors associated with any use of atomic and nuclear weapons. If reason and non-violent options fail, and war starts, the carnage and death must be mitigated, genocide must be stopped...by a strong armed response."

I had discovered so many mysteries through the lenses, and I wanted more answers. "Why do so many humans seem to have such a low regard for life? They brutally kill their own with increasing efficiency, slaughter animals, destroy vast forests and the innumerable species that live there, and kill the fish and other creatures in rivers and seas with their pollution and illegal harvesting. How can they be made to realize what a rare, beautiful phenomena the diversity and nature of life on this planet is?"

"A lack of respect for the sanctity and dignity of life. A lack of knowledge of the importance of only taking life when necessary to maintain a harmonic balance among all life and the planet."

I spoke again. "Many humans seem to believe in a divine being...a God...and worship regularly. But often their thoughts and actions don't reflect the philosophy of their God. Why doesn't religion play a greater role in learning The Truth...in humans becoming enlightened?"

The Wise One paused, leaned her head back, for the first time looked away from me, and stared through the descending rays of light. Finally she spoke. "Religious influence has contributed a tremendous amount of good, but if war is the human's biggest mistake, the planet's greatest irony is the negative effects of religion. Belief and faith in a supreme power...a God, or Spirit, a divine Prophet, and the principles set forth by this power, is at the core of the vast majority of the world's religions. These principles, regardless of the religion, God or Prophet's name or origin, are universally associated with living one's life in a moral and enlightened manner, with great concern for the welfare of others...exactly the principles that if followed by the humans, would allow them to solve the problems you have seen."

"What has happened, Luggalor, is that some religious leaders, and their followers, have used their religion as an excuse to wield power for their own benefit, to indulge their insecurities, ego and greed, in forms of discrimination, persecution, even thievery. More humans have been maimed and killed in wars fought on ostensibly religious grounds than for any other reason. And at the other end of the spectrum are all-consuming petty issues. Many so-called devout individuals and their religious leaders are more concerned with the minutiae of doctrine than the welfare of humankind. Hate born of religious differences and fueled by the twisted, incendiary rhetoric of a relatively few leaders and followers has ruined far too many lives. If all religious leaders would actually live the principles of love, respect the dignity of all life, teach tolerance and giving instead of taking...the same, the only principals, that each of the true Holy Men preached and lived by...religion would take its rightful place in leading the transformation to a world dominated by peace and harmony. But it must only be the principles of the Truth they live by and teach, not distorted remnants of them."

"Cannot a God intercede in the planet's problems?"

"A God has, Luggalor. Humans have been given extraordinary minds and an inherent goodness of the soul, and the planet the necessary resources, to enable them to solve the problems we are discussing. They only have to learn…and love…and care…and give. What more can rightfully be asked of a God?"

It all seems so clear, the logical, so simple and elegant. But perhaps the same dynamics that are lodged in each human's mind…that offer the opportunity for an existence filled with such intense feelings…such passion…such beauty…are the same dynamics which cause so much pain and suffering. Such potent…and malleable minds. A tremendous challenge, managing this enormous potential…for good, or evil. I, Luggalor.

I was silent for a moment before continuing. "There is a great deal of poverty, homelessness, destitution and starvation on the planet. In underdeveloped, poor countries, many of which are wracked by conflict, drought, and other natural disasters, this is tragic but understandable. But there is a large and increasing number of humans living on the streets in some of the planets' wealthiest, most sophisticated societies. Why is this?"

"It should be the responsibility of every society to provide an adequate level of care for its destitute, its infirm, its elderly. Some will always need help. There is no good reason anyone should starve on this planet, or be without shelter, or medical care, or hope. The Truth…embraced and lived by enough humans. It is not complicated."

"But what about those who are not infirm, or aged, but seem to be stuck in those places where there seems to be no hope…no realistic opportunity for them to prosper?" I asked.

"Education and motivation are the answers, but there must also be opportunities available to individuals as they become capable of taking a productive part in society. It is as unreasonable to expect a high school dropout from a broken, ghetto home whose only role models have been wealthy drug dealers or pimps to aspire to a college degree and a job at the bank as it is to expect an illiterate family in a refugee camp in the desert to become productive in a devastated economy. Alternatives to destitution, massive poverty, or welfare states involve giving humans the tools and opportunities to achieve the dignity and satisfaction that comes with providing for themselves, their families, and contributing to their community."

"Once an individual is an adequate provider and contributor, it is perfectly all right for them to want to improve their own lives, to have leisure time and accumulate possessions. But contributing to the greater good of the planet and its inhabitants, and in particular doing no harm, must always be a part of each decision related to improving one's personal situation. It is a state of mind. And comes from finding that quiet place in the mind and soul that is free of the world of ego and illusion. It comes from allowing the understanding of The Truth, of love, that is within each human, to surface and flourish. It comes from clearing the lens of harmful filters, forgiving and healing, then learning and teaching. Irony...again. The contentment and joy that come with living the Truth make it easier and less of an internal conflict to attain success and the possessions and lifestyle that so many seek by the wrong means."

"Why is prejudice so prevalent among the humans."

She continued. "Instilling a sense of self-worth, teaching respect for the basic dignity and equality of all humans, eliminating class systems or the astounding gaps in economic disparity among groups within societies...these are the keys to eliminating the harmful prejudice that is present everywhere on the planet. It flourishes in the minds of those who, because of insecurity, feel a need to perceive others as having a lower status than they do. For humans with low self-esteem, having others to look down on...to feel superior to...is a strong draw. Filters on lenses that cause prejudice form easily."

"Life on this planet is so fascinating...the diversity of plants and creatures, the remarkable intricacy of their structures, and the perfection each displays for its unique, magically orchestrated part in the ecosystem." I could not hide the resignation and sadness in my voice. "Humans pollute the air and water, mine and destroy far more of the forests than is necessary, and constantly interrupt and damage the physical properties and dynamics of their environment. It appears their destruction could eventually include their own species...and in the not too distant future. The problems seem to be increasing exponentially."

Her voice never wavered, and had the effect of a gentle, soothing, flowing river. "Life seems resilient and adaptable to extreme conditions. Within certain localized parameters it is. But the line separating this planet's ability or inability to sustain its' sophisticated, diverse species, including humans, is a fine one. You have seen the devastation a worldwide elevation of just a few degrees of temperature can cause. It will get worse. Extreme drought, flooding, the disappearance of huge areas of coastal and low-lying lands. The disruption of agricultural environments and the ensuing surge in poverty, refugee and political problems. Catastrophic storms, the extinction of millions of species of wildlife...more deadly disease and more wars, as people fight over dwindling and shifting resources. It will affect everyone, from the wealthiest individuals and nations to the poorest."

"Each individual, each leader, must learn everything possible about how they pollute or harm the environment...and how they can help to clean it up. And they must act. The best minds, facilities and resources must be utilized and coordinated to seek solutions. Personal and institutional greed must not override the decisions and actions that will be needed if the environment and life as the humans now know it is to survive. The bottom line must be relegated to equal status with saving the planet. Organizations that harm the environment with their products and services must realize there is as much or more profit to be made through products and services that address environmental problems and alternative energy sources, although the moral imperative for change should be adequate motivation."

"We have talked about many things, Luggalor. And we will talk about more, but perhaps you should eat and rest before we continue."

"But there is so much to learn and it seems time is so important. I am very anxious and would like to continue so I can go back onto the planet as soon as possible and help the humans."

"Will your Council allow you to stay?"

"Yes. The Council decided it would be well worth my staying if I could help. Of course I was very persuasive."

"And what form will you take, Luggalor?"

"I can take my natural form or keep the human form you see me in. If I keep my human form I will remain susceptible to all the emotions, physical dangers, and mortality of the humans. The dangers do not bother me so much, and I love being able to feel what the humans feel. But I would have many more powers in my natural form, and perhaps I could be of more help that way."

Through the rays of light I saw a slight smile cross her face as she began to speak. "Humans are very suspicious, Luggalor, and stubborn. As we discussed, they often go to great lengths to believe only what they want to believe rather than the Truth. A being such as you, in your natural state, among them and trying to teach them...well, it would be difficult. It is a decision you must make, but if I were you I would give serious consideration to keeping your human form. Now eat and rest and then I will return." She nodded toward the table. Once more, it was filled with food and drink.

"It is so strange and contradictory...all the destruction, suffering and death," I said. "And caused by the same beings who can be so kind and caring and giving, who create such wonderful music, beautiful paintings and sculpture, and write such stirring and insightful poetry and prose."

"Yes, Luggalor, it seems strange, but it is understandable when you consider the enormous complexity, capabilities and potential of the human mind. You alluded to this earlier. You are indeed perceptive. The human's thoughts and actions can extend as far into the realm of evil as they can good. The challenge is to focus this vast power on the good." The Wise One looked at me through a long moment of silence, then motioned toward the table.

"How did you come to this beautiful place? Have you always been here?" I asked.

"My ancestors came from a lovely island long ago. An island of the spirit. An island that could not be tolerated by the humans...that was destroyed because the Truth interfered with the world of illusions."

She rose from the chair to the full height of her noble beauty, then blended and disappeared into the rays of light as she walked away.

2015

LONG ISLAND, NEW YORK

New York Times   October 10, 2015

The exquisitely painted autumn forest was serene, its silence broken only by the rustling of a gentle breeze that brought the drifting descent of still more pieces of a growing, patchwork carpet. A delicious, clean aroma filled the clear, crisp air.

"Martin, this is a maple leaf, and this one is from a hickory tree. They are very bright and beautiful, don't you think?" The middle-aged man had a warm, compassionate smile on his face as he spoke to the child.

"Yea, it's bootiful."

"Here, hold it. All these trees will grow more green leaves next spring to replace those that are now falling off. And then they will change into these beautiful colors again next autumn, and then it will be their turn to fall off the trees."

"Look! There's a squirrel. See it running up that tree with its acorn. That's what it will have for dinner tonight."

"Is it a real squirrel? It looks like a gray rat with a tail," Pascal said. "I've never seen a squirrel. My mama kilt a big rat. I seen it and it was bleedin' all over everything."

"All right everybody, time for the ropes!"

"No, please don't make me climb them ropes, Mr. Luggalor."

"They're too high. They're way up."

"Yeah, they's too scary. We'll fall off and be dead."

"No you won't. Now remember what I told you. You're

going to have a rope attached to you and your friends are going to be holding it very tight so if you slip you won't fall. You will each climb up to the platform and your friends are going to help you and keep you safe, and when each of you reaches the top you are going to feel better than you have ever felt, because you are going to help each other and yourselves do something very important."

When their turn came each child struggled slowly up the thirty feet of squares of rope that he had attached between the two trees. They pulled themselves with their small hands, straining for each rung, groping for each uncertain step, crying when they were frightened, or tired, or slipped. A few tried their best to give up until they realized he wouldn't let them. As each of them finally climbed onto the crude wooden platform at the top where he stood and urged them on, then hugged and congratulated them...they screamed and thrust their hands into the air with joy, relief, and pride. There were more tears, and not only theirs. After helping each of them back down by climbing the wooden steps on the back of the tree until he was exhausted, a child clutched to his back each time, the small man in the rumpled khaki pants and frayed plaid shirt asked them to sit on the ground in a circle.

"I want each of you to take one more look around before we go. I want you to see all the wonderful trees and plants and leaves in the forest, and remember the birds and the rabbit and the squirrel we saw. And I want you to remember the things we talked about and what we did."

He paused. "Aretha, can you tell me what you learned today?"

"I learned that all the things in the forest, the um...trees and umm...plants and animals...we must love them all. Just like we need to love our parents and everyone we know...and um...that we'll be happy if we love and take care of everything. And I um...learned I can climb the rope if everybody helps me and I can help them. Can we get a treat on the way home?"

"Who votes for a treat on the way home?" he asked. "Raise

your hands if you want a treat."

Five pairs of small, five and six-year-old hands went up at once as he heard the joyous cries and expressions that are so wonderful and unique to happy children.

"All right, but before we go to get a treat, what do I need from each of you?" he asked.

"I know, Mr. Luggalor," Joe, the smallest and youngest of the group says. "A big hug, right?"

"That's right. I want each of you to give everyone a big hug and then give me a big hug. And I want you to promise to give your parents or grandparents or the people you live with a big hug when you get home. Who promises?"

Again the forest rang with a happy chorus of "I do, I do", as they hurried to embrace each other.

After making sure all the children were loaded and buckled up, Luggalor stepped to the back of the old station wagon and laid his jacket on top of the 'Elect Larry Luggalor 12th District Congressman' signs. He closed the hatch, climbed into the drivers' seat, and began the trip back to the ghetto.

The above is an excerpt from an article that appeared in the online edition of the New York Times, an article giving far more praise for my efforts than I would ever condone, but illustrative of how the actions of only one human might have some small but positive impact on educating the world to accept and live the Truth. I, Luggalor.

www.ingramcontent.com/pod-product-compliance
Lightning Source LLC
Chambersburg PA
CBHW020325260626
47156CB00004B/1375